Whispering Generations

Whispering Generations

Manorama Mathai

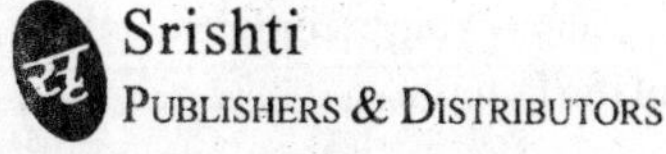

SRISHTI PUBLISHERS & DISTRIBUTORS
64-A, Adhchini
Sri Aurobindo Marg
New Delhi 110 017
srishtipublishers@yahoo.com

First published by SRISHTI PUBLISHERS & DISTRIBUTORS in 2004

Rs. 195.00
ISBN 81-88575-20-8

Typeset in AGaramond 11pt. by Suresh Kumar Sharma at Srishti

Cover design by Creative Concept

Printed & Bound in India

Contents

I

In the Future ...

There is a story waiting to be told. Will I tell it or will it be someone else who follows in my footsteps, as I have followed mother and grandmother, carrying on a family line, its traditions? It is the story of Big House; a house, a family, a way of life in Kerala that has been there a very, very long time and maybe will be there, almost unchanged, for many more years to come...

Big House drowses in the late afternoon sun and appears to dream. Time was and time is flow together as the generations come and go in the old house. Young Mistress merges into Old Mistress and becomes almost indistinguishable. In the future this will be Yuhan's house; Yuhan and Elishuba are the children of young Maria, now the Mistress of Big House, although her grandmother had once been a serving girl in the house.

Elishuba will tell the story and it will be her history, but the story will be of the Big House and the people who had lived within it. It would be the story of her mother Maria, but it would also be the story of her grandmother Kunjam's bizarre death. She would tell of her great grandmothers, one of them the Mistress of Big House, the other an erstwhile servant girl... It will not be her own story that she weaves. It will be the story of Big House, of her mother Maria, who came to the house as a well dowered bride, as others had come before her. Kunjam, whose heart was broken in the Big House and the old Mistress, Elishuba's great grandmother, whose strength of character had carried the family of Big House for so long... The story of Big House is the story of its women who came and went like waves breaking on a sandy shore.

Elishuba had, unlike her mother Maria, married for love half way across the world from Veloorkada and Big House, and on her wedding night she dreamed of her grandmother Kunjam; in her dream she had turned to her bridegroom and said: "Jo, this is my grandma." She had known then that everything went on, that there was continuity, that she had a story to tell.

Elishuba's grandmother often appeared to her. In her infancy, Elishuba had not known who it was, had never been able to separate ghost from real grandmother, who had often enough hung over her cradle. Time had not yet become chronology and so Elishuba never could match the sequence of events against the dates in her young life.

There had always emanated a strange sour smell, not entirely unpleasing. Elishuba had a sharp nose and everyone smelt different, although nearly everyone had about them that heavy aura of coconut oil, applied to body and hair. It was later when that unusual sour grandmother smell had disappeared, thinking back, that Elishuba had known that she was seeing a ghost.

"A ghost is only a ghost when you don't know who it is," she had said matter of factly to her twin brother Yuhan who was not favoured with appearances, in dreams or otherwise, by his grandmother. They said he took after his grandfather

Baben and his grandmother had never hung over his cradle in those few years she had lived after their birth.

Elishuba sometimes felt confused, for in her dreams she was not sure whether her grandmother was she or she was her grandmother. She knew that they held conversations and often, the next morning or suddenly, apropos of nothing, Elishuba repeated snatches of what she remembered.

Sometimes when she said things, made statements, her mother looked at her in surprise. "How could you know...where did you hear that?" she would say in perplexity.

"I didn't hear it anywhere, it's me," Elishuba would reply, equally perplexed.

"She looks like my mother," said Kuri, her father, who was specially fond of her. "That's how it is, I suppose; things go on, life goes on." Almost to himself he had added: "Maybe that is our chance of forgiveness in the life that goes on."

Elishuba had not known what to make of that. She was like a squirrel, paws and cheeks a-bulge with nuts, she carried away ideas, half understood words, dim perceptions, to examine later, to turn over in her mind in the privacy of the attic.

It sometimes seemed to her, looking back, that her grandmother could not have been a happy person and yet... Elishuba remembered Kunjam's mischievous chuckle, a strange feeling of strength that had emanated from her, a sort of zest for life.

Every family had its own mystery; each member of a family

thought he knew the others and yet how divergent would be the way they might describe one another. She knew that almost no one in her family remembered Kunjam as she did. Except, perhaps, her mother. Maria had loved Kunjam.

Elishuba was not really sure what she remembered of her grandmother and what had been woven into her mind by the things that people around her, the family, let drop from time to time. In a family such as hers there were so many old stories and so many old people to tell them; sometimes the same story was told and retold and changed according to who told it. The old uncles and aunts, the servant maids, everyone told stories about the people who had lived and died in the Big House; it was like a never ending tapestry that wove and re-wove itself.

Her aunt Rachie had appeared at great grandmother's funeral; she had, so people said, been quite another person in the far-off past when she had been a young girl living in the Big House. The whispers, the strange expressions on her aunts' faces, made Elishuba imagine that there was something special and interesting about Aunt Rachie. Yet, no matter how hard Elishuba stared at her, she could make out nothing in the least bit strange or interesting about the placid, motherly woman surrounded by her brood of noisy children. Rachie had stood there and wept noisily; she had flung herself on the dead body, asking to be forgiven. Elishuba had been struck by the loudness of her grieving, this almost stranger who was an aunt. She had glanced over at Rachie's children and had been amused to find them looking puzzled and embarrassed. She was glad her mother was not carrying on in that noisy fashion. Some of the relatives murmured from the corners of their mouths, before they quickly rearranged their features in mournfulness: "Trust Rachie to draw attention to herself!"

Elishuba always remembered her great grandmother's funeral. Somehow, she did not remember Kunjam's, her grandmother's, funeral; perhaps this was because it had been a hurried and private occasion. Great grandmother, however, had been given a send-off suitable for the Mistress of Big House. She had lain in state in the front room beautifully dressed with a gold embroidered cloth placed over her, head raised on a satin pillow to hide the bandage that strapped her chin and kept her mouth from falling open. Every now and then someone sprayed the body and the room with Tata's eau de cologne, the strong scent masking but not quite ousting the smell of death. Elishuba looked and wondered and later she had often pondered over it, all the strange things that were said in the service. She could not imagine bedridden great grandma hurtling along in a chariot, eager to reach her home. That is what the priest had said, but wasn't Big House her home and where was that chariot? There were cars there, but no chariots, unless one counted the bullock cart with its pair of white oxen, that was used sometimes to carry things along the narrow village lanes. The priest had also said that if it all came to this (and he had looked at the open coffin before him in which great grandma lay, her eyes closed and her ears and nose stuffed with great tufts of cotton wool) what use was cleverness, wisdom or beauty. Did everything end then when they shut the lid of the coffin? Was everything one had learned and known forgotten? Did nothing remain? These were thoughts that drove Elishuba down from the solitude of the attic and into the very heart of her family for comfort.

The Big House was a happy place for the children, full of lovely scary hiding places, gentle old people with papery soft skins and laps wide enough to comfort a momentary mischance.

There were many cousins and Elishuba and Yuhan especially liked their aunt Rachie's children who were close in age and who had suddenly appeared in their lives. Their great grand mother had been a long time dying and then, shortly afterwards, her maid the one eyed Chauathi, had died too, but quite abruptly. "Gone in a flash, as if she were only waiting to be off," remarked Elishuba's mother and ever after in Elishuba's mind shooting stars reminded her of poor self effacing Chauathi who was quietly cremated with few to mourn the passing of a faithful woman who had been an untouchable but who had been Elishuba's great grandmother's constant companion, who had come with her to Big House at the time of her marriage. What was it that made a person untouchable... Elishuba had often wondered. And how did one know whether one was touchable or not, had old Chauathi minded that she was untouchable or had that made her feel special? It was only much later, long after the faithful old maid had died like a shooting star that Elishuba had learned the intricacies of the caste system. An untouchable could not let even his shadow fall across a high caste person and in order to avoid such a calamity, they were required to herald their approach so that the high born ones could take evasive measures.

Everything had changed from that day after the funeral. Elishuba associated the change with the spring cleaning her mother had given the house. All sorts of objects were moved around; the lovely scary attic was cleared of many old things and yet others went up the rickety stairs to replace them. The Big House, somehow, took on a different aura from that time. It was like an exorcism.

The attic was one of Elishuba's favourite places. It was full of shadows and interesting shapes, a wonderful place to curl up and be alone with herself and as a twin, she needed sometimes to be entirely alone. Lying on a mat directly under the skylight which had been cleaned to allow the maximum possible daylight to slant in, Elishuba dreamed and saw her visions, felt herself part of both the past and a future that could not yet be formulated but that, mysteriously, had already begun.

Her past hung on the walls in the main rooms in front. Old and fading photographs, most of them cloudy and fly spotted, of her ancestors. She had watched when the portrait of her grandmother had been added to the rest. It had been painted from an old wedding photograph and it made Kunjam, her grandmother, look young and vulnerable. That was the way Elishuba knew her from her dreams.

In our past is both our beginning and our end that begins another beginning.

The Big House stands in Veloorkada, which is only a village striving to become a town. It stands at the junction of two roads; one leads to the capital Trivandrum, while the other snakes its way through never-ending villages and bright green paddy fields to Kottayam, the thrusting commercial heart of old Travancore. It seems, as the years pass, that time has stood still in Veloorkada and that it is all unchanging. On the roads droves of schoolchildren, hair oiled, neat in their uniforms, walk to school past churches and temples. Men and women in the traditional white walk on the road, yielding hardly at all as cars and buses filled to capacity drive by, hooting their horns in irate warning. "Whose road is it anyway?" the pedestrians ask each other as they lean to one side, allowing the intruding vehicle to brush past an averted and disdainful hip. And as always, the drivers lean out of their painted trucks that warn everyone to 'keep distance' shake an impotent fist at the pedestrians and enquire if they think the road belongs to their father.

Every time Elishuba comes home to the Big House she feels

the same rush of happiness that she had experienced as a child when she had woken in the morning, gone out on to the veranda and sniffed the morning air and known that something new was on its way.

The air in Veloorkada is a very special blend of smells; there is the hint of fish left out to dry on the sand, the acrid tang of roasting red chillies, the sharp fragrance of coconut toddy brought to the kitchen door to make lace edged appams for breakfast to be eaten with a spicy mutton coconut stew. Cocks crow everywhere, but they remind Elishuba only of home.

It is the same for the rustle of the wind in the coconut palms and the way the sun turns the fronds into gold. When it rains that too is different, lightning and thunder put on a splendid show and then it pours with an intensity that she had never seen elsewhere, swelling the ponds and the river, turning the paddy field into sheets of water. There are memories here. It is a joy to turn a corner and come upon an old tree that she had climbed to pick sour tamarind or small green mangoes. There is a past here but it is hers to take what she wills from it, while there is also a future, both for her and for the Big House...

Elishuba knows all the secrets that have torn her family apart but which have also kept them together; but then that is what families are all about, shielding one another, not betraying the things that have been done out of desperation so long ago, trying instead to protect and to preserve. They might have been protecting themselves but more importantly, they were protecting that complicated thing known as family. Maybe that is what it is all about: being loyal to people who perhaps did not deserve that loyalty, yet being loyal because they were of one's blood and because of an obstinate pride and a primal inexplicable instinct that calls itself love. Out of the debris of despair one builds character.

Elishuba believes that she understands all the things that happened in her family, but she is also convinced that their ways will not be her ways. She will move on because she belongs to another time, but she also knows that many things in her have their roots in her past. Everything, she knows, is linked....

The Big House stirred beneath her as she lay curled up in the attic and she was filled with love for it... the bitterness had been banished and if some sadness remained then it was to Elishuba who loved poetry: "A feeling of sadness, and longing/ That is not akin to pain/ And resembles sorrow only/ As the mist resembles the rain."

Old hatreds, too, all were finished and done with, but within herself was a tapestry of rich and colourful threads and there were magnificent things still to weave.... She would tell the story and it would be her history but the story would be of the Big House and the people who had lived within it. It would be the story of her mother Maria, but it would also be the story of her grandmother Kunjam's bizarre death. She would tell of her great grandmothers, one of them the Mistress of Big House, the other a servant girl...

When Elishuba (unlike her mother Maria) married for love, her grandmother Kunjam, dead long since, appeared in her dream as she lay sleeping within her husband's arms on her wedding night, and Elishuba had said to him: "Jo, this is my Ammachi, this is grandma," she had known then that everything went on, that it was all linked and that she must tell the story of Big House ...

She would tell not only of her grandmothers but also of her grandfather Baben's suicide, of Kunjam's drinking, ending in her bizarre death and the obstinate pride of her great grandmother and the women before her who had kept the Big House and the family going through good years and bad.

II
Looking Back...

1

Tragedy struck the Big House when the youngest son, inexplicably and suddenly, committed suicide. In a joint family and a large sprawling house, a great deal passed muster that might not do so in a nuclear household where people had time and space to observe. So nobody seemed to have noticed the aberration or the sadness that caused Baben's suicide one rainy evening, but everyone was shocked into stillness by the sight of his limply dangling body. No one had intervened when his mother had ordered the tree from which he had hanged himself cut down, herself seizing the axe and savagely inflicting blows to its trunk and branches before she was led away, weeping.

In Maria's memory that death of a beloved son of the Big House was inextricably bound up with the sound of rain thrumming against the coconut palms and the drum beat of distant thunder across the swollen river. Looking back, she remembered that even the perennial whirring of the cicadas had been stilled.

The Big House, it seemed, had always stood there with its

air of solidity that suggested permanence, a fixed and unyielding order of things, with its red tiled gabled roofs pointing upwards, Chinese style. Its doorways were low and the thresholds high, a device that perhaps, discouraged hasty entrance or exit by intruders.

Big House was actually the name of the family that lived within the house but it was applied interchangeably to both house and family. The family had always been landowners, their rice fields and coconut groves stretching away into the far distance merging the green paddy and the blue horizon. All the wealth of the family was in those fields and in the tall coconut palms up whose straight smooth and unyielding heights men climbed, legs wrapped in embrace of the grey bark, inch over inch, to the heights where the coconuts clustered in abundance.

Paddy, coconuts and spices — cloves, black peppercorns, the fragrant cinnamon and green cardamom — from the family's estates, found their way into the large storerooms that stood at the rear of the house where the paddy was stored in huge wooden chests that were miraculously insect proof.

Underneath, in cool rooms, the coconuts were stored, great green globes. In addition, there were cashewnuts, the nut protruding like an impertinent tongue from the astringent fruit; there were mangoes, yams, tapioca, jackfruit, obscenely bulging, guava and from row upon row of banana palms that flourished outside came bananas of all kinds: tiny finger length yellow, large and fleshy red, long greens and yellows, bananas in profusion.

One room, a kind of larder, made entirely of wood, held great jars of salted mangoes, dried fish, crystallized brown sugar and spices, so that there was always something to fall back upon for unexpected guests and these were legion and came always at meal times.

The family of the Big House was a joint family, the generations and many ramifications of uncles, aunts, cousins and more distantly related kin all residing under its roof. And there were servants in plenty, family retainers and casual labourers, to care for the house and its many occupants.

One of these was Maria *Chedathi,* big sister, as she was called by everyone at the Big House, although she had not always been called thus. Years before, too numerous now to remember clearly, (nor was she given to that kind of accuracy, her early life having been spent in hours of endless toil that precluded chronology), she had come to the Big House as a skinny undersized child, big eyed and terrified. Then as she took up her duties, never clearly defined, helping in the kitchen, cleaning, wielding a broom larger than herself, she as the smallest servant girl had been known as Maria *pennu* (girl).

Maria then had looked with awe at the Big House and its inhabitants; the house with its gabled tiled red roof tilting upwards at the sides, its many rooms, verandas, attics, cupboards filled to overflowing with more, it seemed to her, than anyone could want in a lifetime, had fascinated her. The large, heavy dark rafters, beams and wooden struts gave the house a dark grandeur. The inner doors were halved, the upper and the lower halves moving independently of each other, affording privacy at different levels, as when the women leaned over them, keeping modestly hidden behind the lower half. Women did not venture out on the veranda, that was the preserve of the menfolk. Only when she was very old did a woman of the house come out to sit in the coolness of the veranda.

Maria's own home was a two roomed thatched hut in which a constantly burgeoning family ate, cooked and slept. The floor of the hut was of mud, baked hard. In the Big House it was like black marble, a floor found only in old palaces, houses and temples, cool and shining, the sheen owing much to her ministrations on her hands and knees and later, when she outgrew the job, to that of other little girls of whom there was an unending supply from the village.

The people of the Big House had all seemed tall, handsome, fair skinned and lordly. After she moved into the kitchen when, in fact, she achieved the status of being called Maria Chedathi, she saw the young men of the house rarely for they had nothing to do with the kitchen; their food was always served to them by the women of the house, the servants never entering the dining area. But when she had flicked her duster over the carved furniture or swept the courtyard around which the house was arranged, Maria had caught glimpses of the young men of the house lounging on mats, leaning against great big comfortable bolsters and they were to her what film stars were like for more sophisticated girls. She had been known to hang about, assiduously applying duster or mop, in order to get a glimpse of them. Perhaps it was that rather than any culinary aptitude that had led to the Young Mistress moving Maria's nubile presence out of the main house and into the kitchen at the back of the house, separated from it by a long covered passage way where the metal utensils filled with water for pre and post prandial ablutions were kept, one little girl's sole duty being to keep the mellow bell metal shining like mirrors. As Maria told her grandchildren years later, "The Young Mistress, as we called her, was a regular tartar. She was the wife of the youngest son of the house and it was always the custom for the youngest son to inherit the house. The Old Mistress never liked her, I think, but she respected her ability to run the Big House and besides, she produced many sons." Maria added maliciously, "Not that they were any good; when trouble came not one of them was able to do anything. Different from my sons, I can tell you that." To herself she admitted that the youngest son, Baben, who had hanged himself, had been handsome and that her admiring eye had often been drawn to him. And he had certainly looked at her, older than him though she had been and a married woman.

Maria had taken great pride in being part of the Big House –

its storerooms filled with grain from the field, with coconuts, oils and spices; its stables with the oxen for the carts, the herd of cows; the front rooms with heavy carved furniture and cushions of intricate designs on which the Mistress herself had embroidered landscapes and people such as Maria had never seen: crinolined ladies disporting themselves in English gardens, Chinese willow, fruits and flowers far removed from the familiar mango and hibiscus.

Into the crevices and convolutions of the furniture no dust was permitted to creep, first the Old Mistress and afterwards the Young Mistress, perpetually probing with an insistent finger and woe betide the little servant girl should any dust stain that aristocratic hand!

"What would happen?" the children asked and wriggled with anticipation of the familiar answer. Maria's grandchildren loved to hear her stories of long ago, when she was a child as they were, although her childhood world was as far removed from theirs as another planet.

"A stick from the *chool* or broom was demanded by the Old Mistress and later from other small culprits by the Young Mistress and then, after testing the stick for its suppleness, one was soundly thrashed."

"Well," said Maria Chedathi years later, "how else to keep things up?" To her grandchildren, still later, she said: "Oh yes, it hurt all right, the Old Mistress knew exactly where to strike so that it would hurt most and from the way, later on, the little maids cried out, I imagine the Young Mistress struck hard as well. But that made us more careful the next time."

"How dared they? Why did you let them?" Maria's youngest granddaughter, named after her, was passionate, her little frame almost shaking with rage.

The grandmother smiled and touched the little girl's cheek. How could this little one whose life was so far removed from that of her grandmother, ever comprehend the kind of childhood she had led? Instead she went on with her descriptions of the Big House, of the dark smoky kitchen full of women from the first light of early morning to late at night, all busy cooking, grinding spices, boiling great vats of paddy, grating coconuts, making pickles and preserves to fill jars large enough for a person to hide in. She told of serving lunch every day to the hundreds of agricultural workers employed in the fields and plantations and in the vast grounds of the house, who all had to be fed as part of their daily wages.

"At first," she explained, "as a little girl, I was required only to collect and prepare the plantain leaves off which they ate, hundreds of them, to be laid down in rows in front of each person. Then later, I was chosen by the Old Mistress to help serve the meal, ladling out great mounds of rice, each serving had to be exact, the curries and other things in the right places on the leaves. No mistakes were tolerated," Maria explained to her fascinated grandchildren. "Each person watched like a hawk to see that everyone had the same, no one less or more and if anyone complained, it meant sure punishment."

"But didn't they ever praise you, ever say 'well done'?" asked the little granddaughter.

"That was not the way," the old woman replied, "we had our job to do and we did it. There was no question of praise. If we did not do our work properly there were plenty more to replace us. No shortage." She smiled grimly, remembering. She did not add that in the little hut from which she came, her mother had given birth to other children, many of them. All of them needed her wages and the food she brought for them from the Big House, the leavings, of which there was always plenty. "These days," she explained, "there are factories, offices and shops even in the small places and people also go far and wide to find jobs as your fathers did, but in those days, when I was a young girl in Veloorkada, there was only the Big House for a girl like me."

"What else did you have to do?" asked the grandchildren as she paused in her narrative to prepare the wad of tobacco to pop into her mouth. Grandmother had a way of making the past come alive and as every child knows, the best stories are the familiar ones where everybody knows the endings.

Chewing placidly, spittoon conveniently to hand, Maria cast her mind back to those long ago days. 'Funny,' she often thought to herself, 'how much more real those days are than anything in the present. Yet, when these children ask 'how could you'? 'How did you bear that?' I have to wonder at myself. I don't think I was unhappy in those days when I was a young girl but I have no memory of happiness either in the Big House.'

"We had no time for idle thought," she responded crossly, for at such times there came to her an unformulated pain, a feeling that life had not been fair, that much had been missed and perhaps, nothing worthwhile had been gained. Little Maria, her favourite grandchild, who had been watching her face, leaned forward to take her hand and smoothed it gently, placing her young cheek against the worn and work-wrinkled palm. The old woman's eyes misted over and as always she tried to dredge up from the past some jewel of memory to make the children smile.

Life had been good to her, Maria told herself, she had done well, her family had prospered, their hard work rewarded.

The young ones liked the story about the hot sesame seed balls, sticky with sugar, which she had to make; the molten mass had to be taken hot from the pan to roll into balls between one's palms that flinched from the heat. Only little Maria scowled horribly when she heard this and peered solicitously at her grandmother's palms as if expecting them to be scarred. The other children laughed because they thought it funny that their redoubtable grandmother should have been so afraid lest she drop one sesame ball.

Their grandmother smiled with them, but she remembered with awful clarity how her hands were seared by the hot sugary mess ladled from enormous *urulis* and how one little servant girl, a mere scrap of a child, had had her ears boxed for letting one ball fall on the ground. 'And', she thought to herself, 'it was not as though we got any part of those 'oondas' or other sweets we worked so hard to make; oh no, they were not for the likes of us!'

The children of the Big House had never lacked for food of any kind. Yet, they had needed coaxing to eat the delicacies that were pressed upon them, pursued by anxious serving women telling stories and playing games in order to force morsels of food down reluctant throats.

Maria Chedathi had spent hours trying to poke balls of rice, meat and fish between tightly pressed lips and clenched teeth while she tried to distract the children with stories. In her own family, in the hut she returned to every night, her little brothers and sisters flew to greet her, eager to receive the leftovers she was able to bring with her, the cold rice, oddments of meat, fish or pickles. No need to tell stories or follow with food held in an outstretched hand, for hunger was a reality in her home.

Grownups in the Big House had been fussy too. They would eat only one kind of rice and that had to be the finest *chembaavari* and with it a range of curried meat and vegetables to choose from and always there was food wasted. Food left on the plantain leaves was thrown out to the dogs and cats in the yard, the rest was put away in the store room in the clay pots which preserved it for another day to augment another large meal. Sometimes Maria had wondered how people could need so much; people like her parents were content with last night's cold rice and salt fish and sometimes they had not even that, eking out a meal with rice water. But, as she grew up, Maria Chedathi learned to take pride in the prosperity of the Big House and to feel herself part of that well being. Perhaps it was because of the Big House that she had desired more from life, had sought it and had achieved it through her sons.

As a young girl she had gazed with curious wonder at the young men of the house who had seemed like languorous gods. They dressed in silk gold bordered, with gold chains glinting on fair and manly chests; lordly, they never looked at the menials who served them. And yet, Maria brought herself up short, that was not entirely true. There had been one or two who had cast a look in her direction, whose eyes had followed her about as she swabbed the floor, her shapely rump sticking up in the air. The Young Mistress had noticed it too and Maria smiled in spite of herself with remembered satisfaction at how she had immediately set about arranging marriages for her sons and had transferred Maria's sphere of operations to the kitchen.

It was the mother who made all the arrangements. She stood in the doorway while her husband reclined at his ease on the front veranda and she said to him: "Chacko (or Varghese or Thomas) should marry now. It is time." And her husband, as was his wont, agreed: "Yes, yes, you find a suitable girl and we will fix it up."

So the marriages were arranged, grand weddings held and another daughter-in-law came to swell the numbers in the house, immediate family and relatives, distant and close, to be fed, waited upon, massaged with oil and given hot water for long and leisurely baths when they could not be bothered to walk down to the river as was the custom. Only Baben, the youngest son, remained unwed and he seemed in no hurry to find a bride while his doting mother seemed unable to find any girl good enough for her beloved son.

Unfailingly strict and undemonstrative with all her other children, on Baben she had lavished tenderness and devotion that no one, not even her husband, could call upon.

Meanwhile, Maria had found a husband. Her parents were unable to arrange a marriage for her, as was the custom, they had no dowry to give her, but Maria's looks and outgoing personality had stood her in good stead. She had met Eapen who worked in a small printing press in the nearby town and had captivated him into marriage.

The Mistress, Maria remembered, had delayed Baben's marriage, finding all manner of reasons to reject the many brides, rich and beautiful that were offered for him. Everyone in the Big House said that Baben's wife when she came would have a poor time of it. But in the end, after Baben had turned thirty, a bride was finally found. She was reputed to be very fair and pretty and she was very young. That she was also said to be rather clever, nobody considered of any importance. If at all, it was looked upon as a disadvantage, something she might hopefully lose upon becoming wife and mother.

Maria Chedathi now spent less time at the Big House, going there only to help with the cooking. Once her eldest son started earning she was able to take life a little easy. More in the kitchen than in the main house, she saw little of the new bride.

But of course the other servants gossiped, what else did they have with which to spice the day? Kunjam, the new daughter-in-law, was sulky and discontented and as everyone had predicted, she and her mother-in-law could not get on one with the other. Things were not improved by her failure to conceive and the quarrels between the women became ever more acrimonious and bitter.

Baben was moody and withdrawn, never taking his wife's side against his mother. He had always fancied himself as an artist, his half finished oil paintings and watercolours lay all over the house, cherished only by his mother. Maria had come upon one once, undoubtedly of her, depicting a woman coming out of her bath. Although the face had been unmistakably hers, she had wondered where and when he could have seen her thus without her clothes, only a thin cloth standing between her and the gazer. She had stood looking at it, hand to her mouth, horrified by the nakedness. There had been something repellent about it so that she could not recognize the body as hers, not only because she never had looked at herself in that way, but also because there was something strange about the delineation. It was while she stood staring that the Mistress had found her. Her face as she took in the painting had contorted with rage.

"Get out of this room, get into the kitchen where you belong," she had snarled at Maria. That painting was never seen again.

Often Maria had noticed Baben staring at her, his hands held like a frame before his eyes; it had been his way even before his marriage and Maria had always smiled with the satisfaction of knowing that she was beautiful and she had looked at him coyly from beneath her eyelids. "Well," she was to say later in extenuation, "I was young then and knew no better. After all, I had nothing but my looks." Of course, she did not speak of this to her grandchildren, that would never do!

Baben's mother had noticed too and it was then, reluctantly, that she had found Kunjam for her son. "Not before time," said Baben's brothers and sisters, "he is not a boy anymore though Mother treats him like one."

None of them guessed at the truth and if they had, would they have done differently? The Big House family had always kept up appearances, could never endure to be spoken ill of, had to be above scandal. 'What will people say?' 'What will people think'? had always influenced the actions of the Big House family. A 'good name', the Mistress of Big House always said, was the most important thing in the world.

2

Kunjam was young and beautiful. She had come to Big House a bride, full of dreams. Her dreams were simple enough; they were the dreams of any young girl of her class and age, newly married to a handsome young bridegroom whom she did not know at all. She came to her marriage expecting to fall in love with a husband who had never been her lover, a man she had seen only once before he became her husband; as a virgin who had no experience of men, she was filled with romantic ideas and veiled allusions to the married state upon which she had embarked.

Baben, her husband, was a complex person, much loved by a doting mother who could never understand him. With his father there was hardly any relationship, the old man shying away from something unfamiliar about this youngest son and the boy half contemptuous, half afraid, of a man who was both autocratic and childish, who brooked no contradiction yet never permitted rational discussion, stayed aloof.

Baben was idealistic and much affected by the ideas of his

time. He felt keenly the injustices done to the labourers and low caste people of Kerala, injustices perpetrated for centuries by families such as his, the Big House family. In the days following his wedding he tried to speak of these to his young bride Kunjam, hoping to find in her a kindred spirit, a companion, but he was disappointed. Kunjam wanted, above everything else, to love and be loved, to find out who she was and what she might become in the only way she knew: through the eyes of her husband, but this identity Baben seemed unable to give her. In each of them there festered disappointment that, in time, turned for Kunjam into frustrated rage. In Baben, it manifested itself in indifference, all his emotion going into his painting over which he spent hours, excluding his young wife.

He had painted the servant woman Maria and Kunjam had observed him, erupting into a jealous fury that Baben, uncomprehending, treated with contempt. His mother had discovered that painting and she too had misunderstood, had appealed to him not to discredit the family name and the painting had vanished, undoubtedly destroyed by his mother. From that time on, Baben painted in secrecy, hiding himself and his paintings away from the rest of the family, as he did everything else of importance in his life.

Baben's attempts to work for social justice met with no better outcome. His father and elder brothers accused him of fraternising with lower class people, of fomenting strife, of giving the labourers false notions and expectations that could only cause trouble for the Big House.

It had all come to a head with Ellayan, an untouchable whose family had worked for generations for the Big House. They were landless labour to whom the Big House gave a small plot of land to cultivate out of which a proportion of everything it yielded had to be handed back. Ellayan and his family had neither tenure nor any guarantee of good faith. At any moment, for the smallest transgression, they could be dispossessed and at any time, regardless of their own needs, they had to provide labour for the Big House.

These labourers received no cash payment for their back-breaking work in the fields; all they got was a midday meal that consisted of boiled mashed jackfruit (plentiful in every garden), kanji or rice gruel, or kappa (tapioca), also freely available in every home.

Baben demanded that Ellayan be given title to his piece of land.

"Surely", he argued, "after so many years of faithful service the man deserves that much; the land he cultivates is not even a prime piece of property. If it yields well now, that is because of the toil of Ellayan and his ancestors." But the Master of Big House refused; indeed, he and his other sons laughed the idea to scorn.

"What is the matter with you, boy?" roared Baben's father, "are you ashamed of your class and family that you want to fraternise with untouchables and other low life?"

"Perhaps," put in his brother Verghese, "you should spend more time with that young wife of yours..."

"She is certainly better looking than Ellayan's wife and daughters," jeered his other brother Chacko, "and it's time you concerned yourself with planting that field with some children."

The father and the brothers all laughed heartily at this witty sally, but their amusement quickly turned to rage when, Ellayan being indisposed, Baben took up his plough and went to work in place of the labourer who would otherwise have lost his share of the harvest. Poor Ellayan had no sons to help him, every child his sickly wife bore had died in infancy and now there were only two young girls as gaunt and sickly as their long-suffering mother.

"Afraid of their own shadow," Baben said angrily one day in Kunjam's hearing.

"It seems your father and brothers are right", she shrilled at him, "you care only for low life like them. You don't care for me, your wife, you do not even feel that I exist" and she began to cry loudly, bemoaning her loneliness, her regret that her parents had allied her to him.

To his father and brothers, Baben's compassion for the untouchable was inexplicable and unseemly. "After my time," said his father to his older sons, "you boys had better beware because Baben will give away all our land to the labourers who live on it. He is one of these Communists who go about fomenting trouble between people of different classes. They do not know how to leave well alone."

"It is well enough only for us and our kind," Baben replied heatedly, "it has never been at all well for people like Ellayan and his kind. Things will change, they must change. Would it not be better if the change came with good will than by force?"

The old man had looked at Baben with what was almost dislike.

"I told you," he repeated to his other sons, "the boy is a Communist who will cut off his nose to spite his face."Communism, or Marxism as people preferred to call it, had come to Kerala, and was the bane of those who were landowners, since the last thing any of them wanted to do was to share their land with the landless. They were beginning to become anxious, however, for the Marxists were sweeping the polls and coming in to power all over the state.

When Baben went indoors, his mother was waiting behind the doors. "Son," she said, "why do you behave like this and upset your father so much? It is not seemly that you give in to your emotions like that. People should not see you behaving so peculiarly, rushing into the fields and working with our labourers."

"Would you have preferred, Mother, that the poor old man got up and stood in the hot sun and worked although he was not able to? Or do you think he should have stayed on his mat and lost his share?" Baben spoke passionately.

"Cool yourself, son, you should not get so heated up. What

will people think, what will people say?" his mother asked.

"Mother, there are no people here, only you and me," Baben replied, "and I am tired of what people will say, of what they might think. The fact is, I cannot live with myself, what I think of myself, of who and what I am."

"I would have dealt with the matter of Ellayan," his mother told him, not comprehending what he was trying to say, "I would have taken care of matters, there was no need for you to behave so hastily and speak so hot headedly to your father and elder brothers. There are things they do not understand but there is always another way around such matters and we can deal with it, you and I."

"No Mother," Baben's voice was sad, "there are some things even you cannot understand and there are matters you cannot deal with, as you call it. I cannot deal with them myself. I am a misfit and I feel I have no place anywhere."

"How can you talk like that, you who are newly married to a beautiful girl? You have everything you could want. Are you not happy with your wife, my son?"

His mother knew well that everything was not right between Baben and his wife. Kunjam herself had made that very clear to her mother-in-law, who blamed her then and was to blame her for everything that thereof did ensue.

"I am not happy, mother, let us just leave it at that. There is no more to be said and there is no one to be blamed," Baben's voice was weary and he turned away.

That night he went out and drank toddy to his mind's fill with his acquaintances in the teashop and when he returned home he was enabled to make love to his wife and she conceived their child that night.

It did not, sadly, betoken any new understanding, tenderness or love between Kunjam and Baben. An intoxicated man, fleeing from some demon, trying to gain oblivion, does not make a good lover. Kunjam did not know what furies pursued her husband and she did not care. What she did understand was that neither her body nor the love with which she had come ready prepared to her marriage was in any way indispensable to him. His drunken assault on her body did nothing to endear him to her and when he fell away from her and slept stertorously through the night she lay awake and wept, creeping away to another room to lie curled up on a mat, where later her devoted maid who had come with her from her parental home, found her and the two women wept together.

They did not know it, but Baben when he woke up alone in the bed, had wept too and that night was the beginning of the end.

3

One day Maria Chedathi entered the main house to ask the Mistress who still, despite all the many daughters-in-law, held all the keys, to give out the pickling spices from the store. Coming unnoticed into the room she heard Kunjam, her face contorted with spite, saying to her mother-in-law: "Whose fault is it if your son is incapable? He can only do it in his head or if he is drunk and even then it is not with me and any way that does not make babies!"

Afterwards Maria, who had turned and crept unnoticed from the room, was not sure whether the decline of the Big House had actually dated from that day or whether later on she had simply linked the two happenings together. Certainly, tragedy had followed not long after. Kunjam had at last become pregnant but, before the child was born, Baben, its father, had been discovered hanging from the old breadfruit tree at the very edge of the compound.

Maria had wondered then why he had not just stepped into the river on to which the Big House fronted, where the family boats were anchored, why he had not gone just past the family bathing ghat where it was fast flowing and let his body be carried away so that it might be supposed that he had drowned accidentally. That, it had seemed to her, would at least have saved a lot of bother and scandal.

Tongues had wagged, of course. Some said Kunjam's baby was not Baben's and that he had known it. Others held the view that there was a streak of insanity in the family that had tainted Baben, had he not been moody and peculiar, painting strange pictures? That, at any rate, was what Kunjam's family hastened to assert, that the fault lay with Baben. They claimed that the marriage had been rushed through with unseemly haste so that they would have no time to discover the truth about the bridegroom. And, Maria reminded herself, those peculiar paintings he had been so secretive about, hiding them from everyone in the house, had all disappeared shortly after the suicide...

It was for the Young Mistress, (still called that although the old one had long since passed away) that Maria had felt sorry and pity was not an emotion the lady usually aroused in Maria Chedathi's breast. Grieving as she did for her youngest and most loved child, she could not respond with her usual acerbity to the rumours and accusations that were flying around like vultures circling a kill. To blame Kunjam publicly was to bring the family into disrepute and that she would never do. Pregnant Kunjam remained in the household like the irritant grit around which the oyster lays a nacreous sheen; her son was born and brought up as Baben's and the entire family tiptoed around the tragedy, trying to make believe that nothing out of the ordinary had happened.

"It was," said Maria, "as if Baben had gone on a long trip somewhere and everything was waiting for him when he came back so that he would never know he had left.

"No," Maria corrected herself, "his paintings all disappeared, all those funny looking women, bodies naked or as good as, vanished." She ruminated over this, silent for a moment. That was funny, come to think of it; had they been destroyed? If so, she wondered why that should have been; one would have thought the Young Mistress, his mother, would have treasured them even if no one else did.

It was obvious, however, that the heart had gone out of the Mistress. She who had run the family, directed its fortunes, ensured that its storerooms were full, its fields fertile, the labourers overseen, seemed no longer to care. The reins held so firmly in her hands till then slackened.

"It had always been so," Maria explained to her grandchildren, "first the Old Mistress and then the Young Mistress, it was these women who kept Big House going although, if you had asked the Master, he would never have agreed!"

The Master had always lounged on the veranda, content to have the trappings of wealth and power. Occasionally he had made sorties into the rice fields which stretched for as far as the eye could reach; he had shouted at the labour, countermanding orders, coming back to rant at the family, making sudden irrational decisions to uproot the paddy and replace it with sugarcane or, when there was a coconut blight (a not uncommon happening), swearing that he would sell everything and move to the city. Then it was the Mistress who had soothed, made suggestions, given quiet instructions to the labourers. Everyone had listened to the Master, but it was the Mistress they had obeyed.

All this had changed gradually after Baben's suicide. A stroke, the doctor said when summoned. The Mistress had been found lying unconscious on the bathroom floor, her face twisted, unable to move or speak; and after that everything had begun to change. No one supervised the workers and in the house the dust gathered on the precious carved furniture and the Mistress was oblivious to it all.

"Her Chauathi looked after her. She was a faithful old creature but being low caste, she could not do much in the house. Funny woman, spoke little and had only one eye, the other was just a mass of puckers. Some said her husband had gouged out her eye because she was unfaithful. Looking at her, no one would believe that!" said Maria. "She was devoted to the Mistress, came with her to Big House when the Young Mistress came as a bride."

It was left to Maria Chedathi, the most senior of the servants to scold and supervise as the Mistress had done and she did so within the house, seeing to the maids, but her authority could not extend to the fields and plantations outside. Besides, her husband Eapen was ill then and she was preoccupied.

The Master, ever more occupied with his opium pipe, neglected both the fields and the accounts, lolling in his easy chair on the front veranda where the breeze blew coolest, alternately dozing and waking to shout incoherent orders at whoever was nearest. He was content to hand over complete charge to the *kaaryasthan*, the overseer, oblivious that gradually less and less produce made its way into storerooms that had once been filled to overflowing.

"The sons of the house," said Maria, "were never in the way of seeing to anything but their pleasure, so they took their prosperity for granted and went on driving round the countryside in their motor cars, going to the cinema and teashop, while their wives went on buying gold bordered clothes, went on making new jewellery for themselves. They never seemed to notice, none of them ever tried to do anything. First it had been the Old Mistress and then it was the Young Mistress who had kept up Big House; now one was dead and the other was paralysed.

"And Baben's widow never replaced her," added Maria.

Maria paused in her narrative and in her mind's eye she could see the Mistress as if it were only yesterday. "Slowly she went into a decline, she never spoke to anyone and seemed totally insensible." 'The only thing,' thought Maria, but she did not say it aloud, 'was the way she looked at me. Even now, after all these years, it makes me shiver.' Sometimes she had wondered whether others in the house noticed anything, but none of them had commented and Maria had persuaded herself that those baleful looks in eyes otherwise vacant, were a figment of her imagination. Yet, after all these years, she could clearly recall that look and it still made her uncomfortable, so uneasy that even the most juicy wad of tobacco seemed to dry tastelessly in her mouth. 'Had it been dislike?' she asked herself, 'there was no reason; Baben only looked and painted, he never laid a finger on me.'

As if sensing her mood the children would chorus: "Tell about Grandfather."

Maria had married well by the standards of the time, for a girl like her with family obligations and no dowry. But her looks had caught the eye of Eapen. Maria's husband was one of those who had benefited from the arrival of the British in Kerala. "When the first Resident came here to Travancore", she explained to her grandchildren, "he found to his surprise a flourishing Christian community that was so much older than their Christianity. But no one knew how to read the Bible in those days, except the priests, and the common man was quite ignorant of much that is important today. He brought missionaries to translate the Bible into Malayalam and many poor folk got education. Your grandfather's family was among those and they did well. Your grandfather had an English education and he worked in a printing press in the nearby town," she said with pride.

Eapen had fallen into the way of intercepting her as she walked through the rice fields to work at the Big House and their love affair had ripened along with the paddy. Eapen had no close family to thwart his wishes and Maria's parents had been delighted at her good fortune when he had asked her to marry him.

"Often he," in the old fashioned way Maria avoided using her husband's name, "brought home books and magazines from the press and he read them aloud to me. It was not that I could not read, but I lacked his facility with letters and anyway, I loved hearing his voice. It was nice to have an educated man for my husband and he knew English as well."

Theirs had been a happy marriage. They had three healthy sons in quick succession and thereafter she went to the Big House only to cook the food for the day. She did not need to work; her two elder boys had done well at school and had gone to work. She had been determined that education should lift them up and out of Veloorkada. She and Eapen were ambitious for their children.

"They studied well, worked hard and they went up in the world," Maria said complacently, "your grandfather always said that the times would change, were already changing, so that those with brains who were willing to work hard would be better off than those who only had money."

The Big House was shabby, nobody bothered to dust and the little maids who swept the floor were perfunctory with the broom unless Maria Chedathi (known for her sharp tongue) was near or some lady of the house came by. The black floor no longer shone like a mirror and the satin cushions embroidered with ladies in crinoline in English gardens, were faded and torn, the stuffing gaping dismally. The daughters-in-law squabbled among themselves, but none of them shouldered responsibility. And, Maria remembered, Kunjam had started taking a medicine that sedated her so that she seemed to care about nothing.

The Mistress lay on her bed in her room, which the maids were afraid to enter. In fact, the room was cleaned only when someone noticed or Maria Chedathi shouted at the servant women. No one paid any attention to Chauathi, the Mistress's low caste maid. Maria Chedathi's tongue then was indeed sharp as she remembered how the Mistress had been, so fastidious, neat and clean.

"As time passed, the old woman regained some of her faculties and she moved around the house in a wheelchair. She tried to speak but the words did not come out clearly.

"One day as I was cooking lunch, I heard shouting and crying from the back veranda. When I went out there I found Jose," Maria told her grandchildren, "he was the only one of my children still at home with me, being thrashed by the children of the house." Maria still remembered her anger as she had seized her youngest child, and heard one of the boys say, "He's only a servant and servants should be beaten."

It was at this point that the Mistress had been wheeled in by one of her daughters-in-law who demanded to know what was going on. Angrily Maria faced her: "These children have beaten my son, see where the broomstick has cut him" and she held up the child for them to see the bright drops of blood that beaded his shorts.

"They are just children," the daughter-in-law had replied, turning away indifferently, "children will play."

"He is only a servant boy," one of the children said shrilly, "and he was boasting and saying his brothers are cleverer than us, going off to some foreign country. My father says they have to be beaten if they don't do what we the masters say."

Then in a strange rasping voice the Mistress had spoken: "He is right. People must know their place." It was at Maria she had looked and in her gaze was so much malevolence that everyone was horrified by it, failing to rejoice that she seemed once again to have the power of speech. There was a momentary silence and then, Maria had thrown down the large coconut shell spoon with which she had been cooking and said: "Well, that's it then. I'm going."

"And you never went back?" asked the grandchildren.

"No, God was good to me. Your grandfather was doing well and our eldest, little Maria's father, had gone to Singapore where already, he had begun to do well, sending money home. The people of the Big House could not understand that times had changed, that no one could treat other people, make them toil, like that any more. Thanks be to God that I never again had to work in anybody's house."

4

Baben's son grew up accustomed to pity. When he was a child the elders had always said to the other children: "Give it to him, give it to poor little Kuri," and turning away had murmured: "poor fatherless child." His aunts had always sighed theatrically when they looked at him and his uncles gave him whatever he demanded. In fact, the other children of the house used him shamelessly to secure what they wanted and Kuri in his turn learned to use blackmail quite effectively.

At first Kuri had not thought about all these things, had merely accepted that it was natural for him always to get his own way; that even his grandmother, so feared and respected by everyone else, should show him special tenderness. As he grew up, however, he began to question why it should be so. Why, he began to ask himself, was he special?

When Kuri first put this question to Kunjam, his mother, she wept and then began to beat her breast and lament aloud, bemoaning her cruel fate, something he had begun to notice she was apt increasingly to do. It was some time, however, before he learned to connect her tearful behaviour with the appearance and rapid disappearance of a certain type of bottle smuggled in by the maid.

He decided then that the question was better not addressed to adults with their alarming sighs, tears and obvious evasions. It was left to a cousin somewhat older than himself to tell him the truth.

"Your father," he said, "committed suicide before you were born. He hanged himself from the old breadfruit tree down by the outhouses and Grandmother had that tree hacked down. Somehow it started growing again and because Grandmother does not go there and everyone else is frightened of it, it has stayed as it is. Some people said your father killed himself because he did not care for your mother and wanted to live with someone else whom he could not marry; others said it was your mother who had another man."

"She did not, did not," said a tearful Kuri, "my mother is good, she's better than your mother. My father and mother loved each other."

"I'm only telling you what you wanted to know," the cousin replied, reasonably enough. "I don't know what happened. It is only what I've heard people saying when they didn't know I was there."

To Kuri these revelations came as a great shock. He went often thereafter to look at the old breadfruit tree right at the very edge of the compound. He went always in the afternoon when everyone was asleep, when the shimmering midday heat bathed the place in merciless light, banishing possible ghosts. Harshly cut down, the tree had somehow grown again but in a twisted and grotesque fashion with splayed limbs and foreshortened trunk. It never again bore any fruit.

In the house a large portrait of Baben hung in the living room, always bedecked with garlands of dusty paper flowers embellished with red and gold tassels and from the curls of sandalwood entwined in them there sometimes was wafted a faint scent. Kuri, once he learned the secret of his father's death, became fascinated by the picture. It hung so high upon the wall, among all the other faded dusty portraits of ancestors long since gone to their rest, that he could not see it very well although an oil-lamp burned perpetually on the floor below. So, when no one was looking, he stood on a high stool that he dragged over to it and stared up into his father's face. He imagined that his father looked sad, there was a faraway look in the eyes that never gazed back at Kuri. He thought his father looked romantic, like a film star, and he ached with a longing to have known him. Sometimes, when he had made sure that there was no one within earshot, he held conversations with the portrait. Once or twice he imagined his father's lips moved and he smiled.

He looked, too, with new eyes at his mother. He supposed he must always have sensed that her position in the family was ambiguous. No one was close to her and she was intimate with nobody. Now in the light of knowledge he could tell that she was disliked; of all the daughters-in-law she was the only one who never attended on the old lady, his grandmother. If their paths crossed, Kunjam slipped away along another corridor out of her mother-in-law's presence. There were never any salutations on either side, no acknowledgement of each other's existence except for a blaze of hate that momentarily lit up and livened their eyes.

Baben's mother was slowly recovering from her stroke, but was unable properly to express herself. Through her eyes and her bravely struggling speech her family discerned what she wanted.

"Mother," said Kuri to Kunjam one day, testing, "Why do you never go near Grandmother?"

"Why should I?" Kunjam's voice was harsh and rasped like something that has been allowed to corrode with lack of use. "There are plenty of wonderful people in this house to do all that is necessary. Besides, what right has she to mourn like a widow? It is I who am the widow, my child that is fatherless," her voice shrilled and he saw her reach out and surreptitiously drink from what she called her medicine bottle.

Later she came to his room where he sat studying at his table, his schoolbooks spread around him. "Your grandmother never liked me, Kuri," she told him, "you see, your father was her youngest, her favourite son and in her eyes no one in the world was good enough for him. Then when he...when he...died, she blamed me."

"How did my father die?" Kuri asked, not looking at his mother, lest his eyes betray his guilty knowledge of the truth.

"What do you mean how?" his mother's voice was taut like the string of a kite stiffened with shards of glass held tight between two fingers. She came nearer the table and stared at him: "Why do you ask such questions?"

Kuri was silent at first, his head bent over the books, his pencil doodling senseless spirals on the notebook. "Mother," he said at length, "my cousin Moni told me that...that my father, that he..."

"What? That he what?" Kunjam's voice vibrated and the glass cut through the cord and the kite jerked away from restraining fingers, "that he committed suicide? Well, I suppose you are old enough to know the truth. Yes, that's what he did, he was afraid to live, to face himself and everyone in this house has blamed me for it ever since."

"Poor Father. He must have been so unhappy," Kuri almost whispered.

"Unhappy? He? And what about me? Was I happy or have I been happy since? And now," and here she beat her breast with resounding thumps, "now my only child, my son, turns upon me."

"Mother, mother, that's not true. What do I know and how can I dare to turn against you? Please, Mother, please do not cry." Kunjam, however, had worked herself up into a passion and it seemed as if nothing could stop her. Perhaps she needed the outlet he had unwittingly provided. For so many years no one had spoken of the tragedy and although no open accusations were ever made, the blame for her husband's death had implicitly been laid at her door. She had never received any sympathy from her dead husband's family and her own had only too willingly assented to the respectability afforded by her staying on in the Big House where she had existed like a shadow on the fringes of the family, almost totally ignored by everyone, even the children of the house.

Kunjam, never one to guard her tongue, had been silent for too long and now she threw all restraint to the winds: "What do you know about your father and me that you sit in judgement upon me like all the rest of your family? Your father was a useless boy; he mooned around and thought he was in love. He had an idea that he was an artist and must lead a life different from other ordinary men. Oh, he thought I did not know this, but I did. What was he good for? Not what a man is good for I can tell you although it took me many lonely years to piece it all together. Everything was in his head and he was good for nothing."

"Mother please," entreated a horrified Kuri, "you don't know what you are saying."

"No, she does not know what she is saying," said a cold voice behind them and wheeling round, mother and son were confronted by the old lady in her wheelchair, brought in by a daughter whose face looked at them aghast over her mother's head. The old lady's eyes were now no longer vacant and they blazed at Kunjam. "If you ever talk like this again to the boy or to anyone else you will not stay a moment longer in this house. We have fallen low but not that low and I will not let it fall any lower. We should have sent you out then, then when my son died, but I was weak. I am weak no longer and I will not tolerate such goings-on. I forbid either of you ever to speak of Baben." She turned to Kuri and her eyes softened. She beckoned him closer to her chair and stroked his cheek: "You, my child, will never know your father but remember always that he was a fine young man. That is all you need to know, everything else is in the past. As for you," her eyes turned to Kunjam, "go to your room and stay there."

It did not occur to either woman to wonder that they could both love Kuri who was flesh of their flesh and yet feel nothing for one another but hatred. Kuri was to wonder about it later as he failed to reconcile these two women closest to him and, again, when a third entered his life only to remain separate from him while he adored the child she bore him.

5

The Young Mistress, as Maria Chedathi had always called her, although she was now the Mistress, had recovered everything but the use of her legs. A widowed daughter, herself sickly and melancholic, became her mother's arms and legs, but she came back to health to find that the land had been mortgaged and some of the creditors had foreclosed. With the changes sweeping the country, many of those who had once been poor and subservient to the Big House were now its creditors and they were happy to be the instruments of its humiliation, to actually gain ownership of lands that once had belonged to the Big House. As landowners and for centuries the most important family in the village of Veloorkada, the Big House family had done little over the years for the poor people of the area. Every Saturday they gave alms, a few paise, to a stream of beggars and sometimes handed out food and old clothing to some of the poorest of the poor, but it was cold charity and had always been perceived as such.

People remembered the way Ellayapan, the faithful

untouchable labourer had been treated. While the mistress remained insensible from her stroke, the Master in one of his rages, had driven the poor family off his lands.

Very little paddy was now harvested by the Big House, scarcely enough for the family's needs. Money had been lavished on jewellery, cars, electrical equipment; every whim of every son had been gratified and now there was little money forthcoming. The house itself was dilapidated with repair and maintenance put off from one poor harvest to the next, but it was still the Big House. The house and the family name was really all that remained. The sons had been forced to look for jobs in the city and the grand daughters had been unable to marry as they ought because they did not have sufficient dowries. The grandsons were still able to use the family name, the status of belonging to the Big House to marry well, trading on their name; they brought in dowries which, however, slipped like water through a hole into the upkeep of the Big House. The house was like a thirsty giant requiring constant sacrifice, but no one thought of leaving, of giving it up. It had stood for hundreds of years, added to and improved, but always there, its wooden carved walls and ceilings darkened and stained with age and use, its rooms and smoke dark attics filled with the possessions of both the dead and the living, generations of fathers and sons, of wives and daughters.

There were not enough dowries to go round, so one of the girls became a teacher. This was comparatively respectable because the education of girls had long since become an accomplished fact but, nevertheless the Mistress, when her granddaughter came home for the vacations, never made any reference to her profession, to the school where she taught and never enquired about her experiences. The women of the Big House had never worked for their living and to the grandmother it was a horrifying thing that the daughters of her sons had to have jobs instead of husbands to keep them.

This, however, was nothing compared to her humiliation and suffering when another young daughter of the house went away to train as a nurse. Nursing was, to many in those days, a profession adopted only by girls too poor to do anything else. By becoming a nurse the Big House had admitted, it seemed to the grandmother, that the girl did not have a family capable of establishing her in a suitable marriage with the comfortable dowry that opened the doors to matrimony.

The grandmother never again spoke to or of this girl and when anyone enquired (as the mischievous are wont to do, probing a possible wound) she would shrug her shoulders and say repressively: "The young these days are wayward, she goes her own way." And when the nurse sent home postal money orders to her father from Borneo and Malaya and other such places, these were never gratefully acknowledged.

The granddaughter who stayed at home obedient to the dictum that well born girls did not earn their own living, sickened and began to have strange fancies. One day, to the horror of her family, she appeared bearing on her hands and feet the marks of stigmata, the marks of the Crucifixion. No amount of scolding or blandishment could make Rachie admit that they were not genuine. She simply showed them the marks and smiled beatifically.

Rachie had been brought up to believe in her own importance as a member of the Big House family. She had grown up believing that her destiny was marriage and she had been led to believe that in the fullness of time a net would be thrown that would trawl up a bridegroom for her from a family that would be wealthy and highly placed like her own. Her future husband would be good looking, loving and charming. They would have children and they would live happily ever after. It was what the servants had told her as they put her to bed at night and it was what her doting mother had reiterated. It was also what she had seen happen to her older sisters and cousins.

Until her uncle Baben took it into his head to commit suicide and the family fortunes dwindled. By the time she was grown and ready for marriage it was a problem to find the kind of dowry she needed. Rachie was not particularly good looking; 'so-so' was how some described her, others less charitable, called her plain.This, coupled with gossip about her uncle and her aunt Kunjam, meant that a larger than normal dowry was required. Rachie was deprived of her destiny; she developed religion instead, saying her prayers very ostentatiously and reading the Bible at all hours. She went, chaperoned by her maid, to every possible prayer meeting. Then had come the day when she had developed the 'stigmata' on her hands and feet and on her forehead. They were the marks of the Crucifixion and they bled as she entered the room where her family was gathered and held out her palms for them to see. On her forehead were scratches that might have been made by a crown of thorns. The family may not have been entirely surprised but there was no doubt that they were not pleased by these manifestations.

The family doctor was summoned. He could find nothing wrong with the girl, so he talked a great deal about tonics, healthy pastimes and hinted delicately at emotions connected with puberty. He scrupulously avoided the word hysteria and no one in the family admitted it either. Rachie was watched and all knives, blades and sharp instruments were kept away from her, but to no avail. The marks continued to manifest themselves. They all knew what Rachie needed but no one put it into words. As usual, it was left to Kunjam to voice what no one desired to hear:

"The girl needs a man. Every girl needs a man, what else is there for her? But what she needs is a true man, a lusty one, not a poor imitation, afraid even of himself!" She laughed mockingly, her eyes on her mother-in-law, before she left the room on her faithful maid's arm, her maid who always waited in the shadows, ready to come to her beloved mistress's aid. The family heard her chuckle and they all knew Kunjam had taken her so-called 'medicine'.

"What we need," the old lady said to her sons, "is a really rich girl, perhaps an only child who will have all her father's money for herself."

The sons waited in silence, eyeing their mother, for they knew that she never spoke idly and she went on: "I hear that in the next village someone has recently come back from one of those foreign countries where they all go to make money, Persia or Singapore, I cannot remember which. I am told that they have plans to build a grand large house such as we have not seen in these parts. As they are upstart nouveau riche they will jump at the chance of an alliance with our family." She looked at her silent sons and went on: "There is an only daughter, an only child. If she has the Big House what need will they have for any other house? Let them rebuild this house and the estates for her. Unfortunately, families like ours do not have the kind of money these nobodies have made by going to other countries, doing God alone knows what. It is the only way out for us, I am sorry to say. It is of Kuri that I am thinking; he does not grow any younger and it is high time he was married before..." she broke off momentarily and the pain in her face told her listeners that she was thinking of Baben.

"I want you, his uncles, to find out everything you can about this family and the girl. If she is pretty and the family background decent, I am willing to consider a proposal."

The sons immediately set about making investigations in

the village. This involved sitting in the teahouse with their special confidant, a man named Chandy saar. Saar was a form of 'sir' and had come to be part of this gentleman's name because he had at one time taught at a government school in the faraway metropolis of Madras. Since his retirement, Chandy saar had taken an active part in the doings of Veloorkada, functioning as marriage broker, financial adviser, interpreter of news (as a sophisticated erstwhile city dweller he felt that he knew more of world affairs than the villagers of Veloorkada). His wife, often out of patience with him, wished that he would devote more of his time to the business of running his own family affairs. But Chandy saar was not a man to be deterred by mere wifely sneers.

"What you do not understand, woman," he told her, "is that I am a person of some importance and they value my experience of the world. It is only right and proper that I should give them the benefit of my experience." His wife sniffed, long and expressively, rolled her eyes and muttered that if everyone ran around as he did, giving other people the benefit of their experience, few families would survive. Chandy saar ignored her. Now, seated in the teashop with the sons of the Big House, they asked him:

"Chandy saar, what do you know of this very wealthy family that has come to Palliseri?" Chacko, the eldest son of the house, added, "They have it seems only one child, a daughter."

"Of course, of course," replied Chandy saar, who had never

till that moment heard anything about this family, "very, very rich, from Singapore, I think."

"Oh? I thought it was Persia," said Verghese, the second son of the Big House.

"Persia, Singapore, Malaya, it is all much the same thing," responded Chandy saar with a disregard for geography that made one hope that this had not been the subject whose mysteries he had imparted to eager young minds in years gone by. "Yes, yes," he went on, wagging his head and shaking his legs in a manner calculated to make one feel mildly seasick, but which meant that his interest had been engaged, "what is it you want to know about this family? Oh, I get it, the only child, somebody told me it is a daughter."

"It is a daughter," said Chacko, "I just told you so."

"Tchk, tchk, of course, I knew the only child was a girl and of course, I know also that she will be getting not only a big fat dowry, but also everything her father owns." It was this sort of inspired guess that had led to Chandy saar being so often applied to, for knowledge he did not actually possess.

"Well," said Chacko, "can you find out for us where this family comes from and what exactly it is that they have? We need to make enquiries about the girl as well."

"In that case," stated Chandy saar, who was not nearly such an altruistic fool as his wife thought him, "I will need some money for expenses. It is nearly the end of the month and my pension is not due for some time. I will have to take a taxi to

Pallisseri and back and of course, this will take the better part of the day, so..."

The sons of the Big House might have fallen on hard times but their habit of lordliness remained largely unimpaired. They, therefore, shared out between them what they had and handed the money over to their friend. "If it is not enough for the taxi maybe you can get a ride on a bullock cart and we will see about the expenses later," they said with grandiose vagueness. In former and happier feudal times, they had not needed to concern themselves with such petty and sordid details. The family retainers had always known what to do; they were told to go and they went. Alas, life was not nearly so simple now. The brothers sighed for their carefree youth when life had been simple, life had been good. "There is nothing like the good old days," Chacko remarked to his brother who wagged his head in contrapuntal assent.

Chandy saar, who had no intention of demeaning himself by travelling by bullock cart when there were more modern and comfortable means of transport available (and for which he had no need to pay) departed on his errand early the next morning; "Before," as he said to his wife whom he awakened to sustain him with coffee and *appams*, "the heat of the day addles my brains and I can get a ride with neighbour Thomas who mentioned to me the other day that he was going to Pallisseri to see his uncle. He will be coming back in the evening and I shall return with him." Of such dealings was the stuff of greatness.

6

It might have been noticed by those who were unused to such matters that Chandy saar had been given few if any details to help him in a quest which to many would appear like the proverbial wild goose chase. Neither Chandy saar nor, when he had imparted the matter to him, his neighbour Thomas, took this view of it. Pallisseri was a medium sized village and given the putative wealth of the family being sought, it had to be supposed that they must stand out and be known to most of the inhabitants.

Thomas, in addition to being an obliging neighbour and good samaritan, took Chandy saar with him to his uncle's house where that gentleman was pressed to stay for lunch which, after a show of initial reluctance, he partook of very heartily indeed. All the time representing himself as one who was ever ready to give up his own convenience to help others, even rising early and travelling without breakfast to Pallisseri with which words he demolished for the second time and in a different way, the *appams* his poor long suffering wife had risen before daybreak to make for him. And as always in this world, such behaviour was rewarded.He had to proceed no further because his hosts knew everything he needed to know about this wealthy new family in their midst. Knowledge that they shared along with their meal.

"They are good people. Mathu, as we call him, is a widower with only one child, a girl. His old mother lives with him. He and his younger brothers went to Malaya when they were young and they all did well there, but Mathu is by far the richest. They say his mother once worked for a big family near here but I don't know the truth of that. His father was an educated man of good family, that much I do know, as we have some distant connections by marriage with them."

"How did they come by their money?"

"Rubber and tin. Mathu still goes back every now and then to see to his business but he intends now to build another and even more modern house here for his daughter to live in after she is married and from what we hear, it is going to be the grandest house that anyone has seen in this country."

"And the girl? Is she fair and good looking?"

"Good looking enough and she is fair-ish, but with money like that who will give a damn? It would not matter if she was as black as a crow or one eyed," put in the lady of the house as she leaned over to stoke up Chandy saar's empty plate. Her husband frowned but Chandy saar nodded; it was true enough. Money, plenty of it, could whitewash anyone or anything. It was only a love marriage that required beauty to fuel the relationship. He frowned; there was something wrong about that reasoning, he felt, but could not quite put his finger on what it was. Seeing the frown, his hosts imagined that he was not pleased and they hastened to reassure him that, unnecessary though it might be, the girl in question was definitely pretty and not at all dark and far from being one eyed, she certainly had the usual complement of all necessary limbs.

"Who is it you are negotiating for?" asked Ammu, the lady of the house.

"Ah, now that is still highly confidential," said Chandy saar, " but," as she leaned over and planted another large dollop of fish on his plate, "I can tell you this much, the boy belongs to the finest family in Veloorkada, an old and illustrious name but alas, badly in need of money these days." With which words it was made crystal clear to everyone that it was the Big House that was involved.

The next step in the day's proceedings required that Chandy saar see the family in question and their environment in order to be able to report more accurately to the Big House. Thomas and his uncle looked at one another and considered the matter. The lady of the house watched them for a moment before she spoke: "Let me suggest one thing. I am supposed to go there one of these days to collect some tender mangoes for pickling. I can take Chandy saar with me and he can get a look at the house and meet whoever is there."

"But," objected her husband, "Mathu is not there, he has gone to Singapore."

"It does not matter," said Chandy saar, "at this time all I need is to get an idea of their circumstances, all quite unofficial at this stage."

In the end all three gentlemen elected to accompany the lady on her errand of collecting the special small pickling mangoes. Thomas was called upon to drive them there, this it being supposed, giving them all a reason for the expedition.

When the car turned into the compound it was immediately clear to Chandy saar that the circumstances of the people who lived there were more than merely comfortable and he rubbed his hands, nodded his head and clicked his tongue in vicarious pleasure. The house was large and stately with a many columned portico standing out in front. The front garden was extensive with crotons of every variegated hue and many carefully cultivated flowerbeds, while to the rear there were coconut palms and other forms of cultivation. As the old Austin swept up the drive an elderly servant ambled round from the side of the house. "The Master is not at home," he said, looking them up and down, "who is it you have come to see?" Then he recognized the lady. "Was it today you were supposed to come for the mangoes?" he asked somewhat superciliously.

"*Eddo*," said Chandy saar before any reply was forthcoming, "you take yourself inside and tell your mistress that there are important people from Veloorkada here to see her." When the manservant, abashed by the less than polite salutation and tone of voice, which had clearly marked him as the inferior, had gone in, Chandy saar turned to his companions.

"I see," he said genially, "that here the master's wealth has turned the heads of his servants and now they think they are the equals of everybody. One has to be very firm with that sort of fellow or they will climb on your head. Fortunately, I know just how to deal with such fellows." Had he been seated, he would surely have shaken his legs as a mark of his pleasure with himself; as he was standing, he contented himself with wagging his head.

An elderly woman came out into the veranda and peered out at them, shading her eyes from the glare beyond. "Oh, Ammu, is it you? What brings you all here in this heat?" Her eyes went from one to the other and she was unsmiling. It was left as usual, for the irrepressible man of the world Chandy saar to speak: "Perhaps we seem to you, *Ammachi*, like people who have come round collecting for the church or some other charity. Let me assure you, it is no such thing. I am visiting here from Veloorkada...perhaps you have heard of the Big House and this is my neighbour, Thomas. We are on our way back to Veloorkada and decided to drop Auntie Ammu here on her errand to collect some mangoes."

It was immediately clear that the words Veloorkada and Big House had made some deep impression on the lady. She stared keenly at Chandy saar but clearly was unable to place him and yet her curiosity had been piqued. "Why don't you all come in and have something cool to drink while I send the servants for the mangoes?"

Behind her back, as she turned to lead the way into the house, Chandy saar exchanged a look of triumph with his companions.

"So," she said, when they were all seated in the very opulently furnished sitting room, "you are from the Big House you say?"

"In a manner of speaking. Chacko and Verghese, the sons of the house, are my good friends and you might say that they look to me for advice in every little matter because they value my vast experience of life in a big city and as a moulder of young minds. I was a teacher in Madras for many a long year."

"And what of the Mist... the old lady and old man?"

"The old gentleman is dead, he was bedridden for a long time and died some years ago. What you might call a merciful release," Chandy saar said pontifically.

"I should imagine he was lost to his opium before that."

"Ah, so you know the family," asked Chandy saar leaning forward and starting to wag his legs, a sure sign that he was beginning to enjoy himself.

"I knew of them," the lady replied indifferently, "it was many years ago." Then she leaned forward and her voice sharpened: "What became of Baben's wife and child?"

"Perhaps you were at school with one or other of them from

Big House?" asked Chandy saar, trading question for question.

"No," she replied shortly.

"Oh! Well, poor Baben's widow lives there and is er… not well. The son, Kuri, is a very clever boy and good looking too. In fact, funnily enough, it is because of him that I am here today. His grandmother has entrusted me with the task of finding a wife for him."

"Indeed," said the old lady, "and where is it you are looking?"

"It could be here," and Chandy saar looked arch, "but I must tell you that a bride for the Big House must have everything, no ordinary girl will do."

"Is that so?" she seemed amused. "Yet it seems that the Big House now is big in name only, they have no money at all."

"This, unfortunately, is true but if you untie a golden bell from around an elephant's neck it does not turn into a mouse. An elephant is an elephant even without its trappings. It is the same with the Big House," Chandy saar was well-known for such remarkably pithy sayings.

It was at this moment that the servant entered with the mangoes. The lady of the house rose. "There you are then, Ammu, take your mangoes." It was clearly a dismissal, but as she began to usher them out she detoured to a bureau that stood to one side of the room on which was arrayed a number of framed photographs. She picked out two and held them out. "This is my eldest son Mathu who is away in Malaya and this is his only child, my granddaughter Maria." The photograph in its heavy silver frame was passed around. The face that looked out at them was undoubtedly pretty but more interestingly, from the point of view of those present, the girl was bedecked as far as the eye was permitted to go, in what appeared to be a most satisfying amount of heavy gold jewellery. This interesting detail was brought to the attention of the men by Ammu who pointed with a discreet but knowing finger. It clinched the matter as far as material considerations went. The girl was undoubtedly wealthy and she was not bad looking either. Chandy saar rubbed his hands together and the others were excited too. Match-making was a heady business.

7

Maria Chedathi watched her unexpected visitors depart and she chuckled to herself. There was no doubt about what had brought them to her house with the flimsy story of the mangoes. That Chandy saar was obviously a go-between for the Big House. How times had changed, she mused, when the Young Mistress could stoop so low. The Big House must indeed have fallen on hard times to seek marriage with her family. She had no doubt that they knew her identity. Except that now it was her family that had the money while the Big House family, from what she knew, had lost everything it had.

Unconsciously, Maria Chedathi straightened herself. Nobody called her 'chedathi' any more. She was 'Amma' to her family and had various respectful honorifics from friends, neighbours and servants. She was now a woman of considerable substance, a wealthy woman, not to put too fine a point on it.

Her sons had all done well and the oldest had amassed a fortune in Malaya by dint of hard work, shrewd business sense, perseverance and unremitting thrift. She often thought that of all her sons Mathen was the one most like her with a capacity for hardship, which in his case, had been amply rewarded. The only thing he lacked was a son. His wife had died trying to produce a male heir but all she had left behind was a daughter Maria, named for the grandmother, in whose fond eyes the child was worth a clutch of sons. Alas, society did not deem it so; it was a son that carried on the family name, a boy that brought honour and prestige to a family. A girl merely passed through and helped to create another family elsewhere. The old woman sighed; she had always hoped that their wealth could persuade some nice young man to become 'dattu', take the name and lineage of his wife so that their family could continue through Maria. Strange was the reasoning of those who believed fervently in one thing or another. Everyone was obsessed by something. But now, if little Maria were married into the Big House, what a triumph it would be!

Little Maria, as she was called, had grown up very differently from her grandmother. A child of her father's prosperity, she had known neither hardship nor privation of any kind. Not for her the need to earn her own living in the way her grandmother had done. Reared far away from her native land in British Singapore, she had grown up imbibing other values, different mores.

Young Maria, deprived of her mother at an early age, had grown up cherished by her father whose only child she remained since he had refused to entertain any suggestion of remarriage.

She had grown up in the care of her grandmother to whom she was devoted. It was she who as a young girl had so resented the hardships her grandmother had recounted in her tales of long ago when she had been employed at the Big House. The grand daughter had as a result, grown up with an implacable hatred of the people who had in her view been cruel to her beloved grandmother, even though the grandmother herself had never admitted that word, had always tried to make her grandchildren see that it was but the way things had been then.

Young Maria had, at one time, even fancied herself a communist and thought that she might work to bring about the downfall of people like the family of the Big House. Some of her early dreams had been of herself as a crusader for social reform, setting free from slavery people like her grandmother. However, she had enough common sense to see that her own personal fortune (which she had no intention of sharing) and her comfortable home in the affluent suburb of Tanglin, was incompatible with what she was trying to be. Besides, the dreary conformity and grey passion of the comrades she encountered had deterred her, much to the relief of her father and grandmother.

Maria's father was in the process of winding up his business in Malaya, preparatory to settling down in India. He had married late having struggled first to establish himself and help his younger brothers to make a place for themselves as well.

While the British, who ruled Singapore, lived a life of leisure and luxury, the efficient Chinese, Indians and Eurasians slaved. People like Mathen had become indispensable to the British bosses and then had managed to gain a share of the wealth that was there for the taking. Not for him the leisurely life; unlike his English bosses, who whiled away half the morning in a leisurely fashion consonant, they felt, with the climate, Mathen started work early in the morning and worked late. He never stepped out to Robinson's or John Little's for a cup of coffee or for a gin bitter and he did not frequent the Cricket Club or the cafes, which lined Jalan Besar Road or Lavender Street. Certainly, he never frequented the infamous Bugis Road and other low dives where many men went.

Mathen often said that he had never had youth to enjoy and so he would not make the mistake of frittering away his later years in endless toil which he needed no longer. His daughter had teased: "You don't know how to enjoy yourself, Appa, you have had no practice at it. You only know how to work." Then she had frowned: "Besides, I don't see why we can't stay here where all our friends are, where we have a good life."

"Then let me explain why," Mathen had said calmly. "This is the country where I came to make my fortune..."

"And thanks be to God you succeeded," his mother intoned piously.

Mathen inclined his head in acknowledgement. "But we do not belong here. We are outsiders and our real place is back home."It was the age-old cry of the unwilling immigrant, the expatriate who never puts down roots, of Naomi and Ruth weeping amid the alien corn. "We will go back where we belong, where we speak the language and where we shall be respected." There was nothing of the Prodigal Son about Mathen who felt that he indeed deserved the fatted calf and ever since he had first begun to make money, this was the dream he had cherished, shared with his mother, of a triumphal return home. Of what use was money and worldly possessions in an alien land? The truest satisfaction came from the admiration of one's peers, one's own people, especially when one had silently suffered humiliation.

"Where we were not respected before, the country you had to leave in order to find paying work, where grandmother had to work as a servant and be treated as one." Maria's voice was tremulous; she did not want to leave the country of her birth where she had friends, identity and freedom of a kind she knew she would not get once ensconced in a village in India.

"You think too much about the past and it has nothing to do with you," her grandmother had chided. "Your father and I and your uncles are important people in Pallisseri and if you marry well you and we will gain importance. Here we can never belong in the same way."

"I belong here. I was born here, I hardly speak Malayalam, I have friends here. I don't know anyone in Pallisseri..."

"Which is why," her grandmother had explained placidly,

"you and I are going first, to get settled there, before your father comes to join us. Oh, I am looking forward to it."

"Appa," Maria had cried passionately, wheeling on her father, "that's not fair. You never consulted me. Surely I should have a say in what concerns me or is my life not my own?"

"Now, now, my little girl," Mathen began in a conciliatory tone for he could deny his little daughter nothing, but his mother interrupted: "That is not the way for you to speak. You have been too long in this free and easy society with your Rose, Paula and Su Lin and it is high time you learned your own ways. You cannot stay here forever and marry some Chinaman or Malay, you know you have to go back and marry one of our own people."

"One of our own people," Maria muttered rebelliously, "as if there are not enough of 'our own people' right here. If I wanted to marry one, that is."

"You will marry who we tell you when the time comes and God willing and that's the end of it," her grandmother was imperturbable. "Don't you think your father and I want only the very best for you? You will marry into a grand family and we will be so proud of you. Isn't that what your poor father has worked so hard for? Now, does my little girl want something special for tea?" The affection was hard to resist and Maria knew that in the end, through a combination of filial love, lack of any definite direction and a habit of comfortable dependence, she would do as her family wanted.

Yet she had made half-hearted attempts to turn them from their purpose of leaving Singapore for Pallisseri because she knew she was going to be bored out of her mind in that village without the friends she had grown up with and would miss the sights and sounds of familiar Singapore.

Maria had not succeeded in those attempts (although, unbeknown to his mother, she had extracted from her father a promise that should Pallisseri prove too terrible to endure, she would be allowed to return to Singapore). Her friends had smiled cynically when she told them.

"You know what you Indians are like la," Paula had said.

"Almost as bad as us Chinese," Su Lin had added.

"Marry someone old and rich who will let you do as you please la," Rose advised, "or marry someone very poor and young who will agree to come back here with you to make money as your father did." It was sound advice; a pity that it could never be used on a man who considered that family and status counted above all else, who would never dream of leaving his birthright behind while he sought adventure in a far off land. Only the desperate and the valiant left everything familiar behind them to go to look for what their spirit craved. Maria's husband would dream of adventure, but he would never need or consider doing what Maria's father had, especially since Maria would come to him and bring the requisite money with her.

8

Old Maria thought about all this as she stood there watching her guests chug down the drive in their ancient car. She felt strangely excited; what an extraordinary thing if little Maria were to end up married into the Big House. What a triumph that would be for her and for her son! Loving grandmother though she indubitably was, at that moment she thought of her granddaughter not at all except as an instrument.

She remembered as if it were yesterday her youngest son being beaten by the children of the Big House, of the old lady saying in that strange raspy voice that servants had to be beaten. She remembered her husband Eapen saying, "It will all change one day. Education and opportunity level society faster than anything else. Our sons are clever and they are hard working. Twenty, thirty years from now they will be the equals of anyone, from the Big House or elsewhere." She smiled a little sadly. Eapen had not lived to see the really good times and he would never see little Maria mistress where once that other Maria had been servant.

Chandy saar, meanwhile, was congratulating himself and his companions on the meeting they had so cleverly contrived. "There is no doubt that the old woman knew what was what," he said. "It was very obvious that she was more than just interested. Didn't hesitate for one moment, almost pushed that photo of the girl into my face."

"But," objected Ammu, "are they, the people you are representing, not going to want to know more about the girl's family? Although they are now so rich it is said that the old woman's family was of very low origins."

"It is money that is crucial here," replied pragmatic Chandy saar. "If there is enough of it, eyes will close to everything else. You mark my words."

It looked as if he was right.

The sons of the Big House carried everything that they had gleaned from Chandy saar to their mother who sifted carefully through it all. "The grandfather," said one son, "appears to have been of good stock, if poor, but no one seems certain who or what the grandmother is. Some hold the opinion that she is of a good family that fell on hard days but others hint that she may have been a servant before she married."

Their mother pondered this and decided that most of what she had heard indicated an undesirable connection, the sort she would not have even considered in the old days. Nevertheless, the money, which seemed to be abundant, remained eminently desirable and necessary enough to make the rest of no account. It was what Big House was most in need of.

"We shall proceed in the matter," she told her waiting sons, "get Chandy saar to sound out the family." This meant that he would hint that a proposal from them would not be unacceptable. Custom dictated that a marriage proposal had to be made by the bride's family.

Chandy saar went happily off on his errand which not only rescued him from the mundane household tasks his wife seemed to think were the province of a man who had retired, but also endowed him with prestige as befitted one working for the BigHouse, entrusted with such a delicate and confidential matter as marriage negotiations. He was most cordially entertained by the girl's father and uncles, who listened to him with attention and apparent respect. He returned to Veloorkada well pleased with himself and informed the Big House family that they would soon be entertaining a proposal, but to his chagrin and that of the Big House, silence reigned thereafter. No proposal was forthcoming. Chandy saar was crestfallen, unable to explain the disconcerting inactivity after he had described the enthusiastic reception he had received.

The old lady began to take umbrage; who did these upstart people think they were? She recognised that they were playing a game common in matrimonial negotiations of trying to enhance one's value by delay tactics. After all, she thought indignantly, what did they have but money? Neither name nor breeding, their origins obscure if not positively dishonourable. There had been a time when she would never have stooped so low. However, as the expense of maintaining the Big House mounted, as she looked at her unmarried granddaughters, some earning their livelihood like girls from any ordinary family, while others like Rachie sickened and became hysterical, lately showing signs of stigmata on hands and feet, given to seeing what she called visions, the old woman's spirit weakened. The girls had to be married off, something had to be done about it all before everything became too late, before trouble struck. Girls left brooding about the place were dangerous, boded no good. She could not endure the sight of Rachie's bleeding palms and feet, she recognized them for what they were: a plea for fulfillment. Rachie and the other girls needed husbands. Pride had to be swallowed; maybe one day, when the Big House was restored to its former glory, but that time was not yet... Chandy saar was sent for once more and despatched again to Pallisseri.

This time he brought back a response of a definite kind. An uncle of the girl accompanied him who was charged with making the formal proposal of marriage. This was accepted and the financial arrangements were discussed. It seemed right and proper to everyone concerned that because the bride's family was lowly, they should pay dearly for the privilege of marrying into the moribund Big House.

Although unstated, it was the old lady's intention that the

dowry Maria brought with her should enable two girls of the house to be married; that the Big House should not only be restored to its former glory, but be maintained with Maria's money so as to restore them to their former position as the most important family in that region. So the final figure named as Maria's dowry was over large by ordinary standards.

The bride's family quibbled somewhat. That was expected; after all, anything bought and sold is subject to fierce bargaining and marriage was no different. Marriages may be made in heaven but the pre-nuptial negotiations are made here on earth; before the priests turn it into a sacrament with their chanting and invocations, marriage is a business contract. In the end, however, the main terms were agreed and Kuri was, as he said bitterly, sold to the highest bidder. The last straw was that the money did not pass into his hands. Mathen was too shrewd a man for that and he stipulated that the bulk of the money would be placed in the bride's name. "We have to safeguard our little one's future," he said to his mother.

Kuri could not gainsay his grandmother who pointed out to him that it was his duty to marry advantageously. His mother, even if she had wished to do so, had not the position in the household to speak for him; besides, between mother and son there existed no closeness, there had been none since that long ago encounter when she had railed against his father. Kuri could not talk to Kunjam of what lay in his heart, there was no one to whom he felt he could turn.

In any case, poor Kunjam was what was known as a secret drinker; in fact, it was no secret except that her maid brought the liquor to her in secret and she drank it in secrecy. The maid obtained the coconut toddy from the man who came to harvest the coconuts from their proud heights. The oblivion thus bought and gained was obvious to the whole family but, as in so many things, silence bought the right to turn away.

Kuri was like his father, everyone said. He thought this meant that he was artistic and idealistic. What they meant was that he was dreamy and impractical, the neighbours saying quite openly that he lacked 'push' which was, it seemed to everyone there, a very necessary quality for modern day living. Writing poetry was, they all agreed, a waste of time and not a manly pursuit. Writing poetry, although no one said this aloud, was akin to Baben's paintings and look where that had led!

His father's suicide had assumed in Kuri's eyes a romantic aura because he had convinced himself that Baben had grieved for an unattainable love which had led to his laying down his life rather than living without her. Kuri wrote poems about the breadfruit tree from which his father had hanged himself and he turned that poor grotesque tree, now twisted and barren, into a sort of shrine to love and unfulfilled longing. Nobody thought to tell him that these were unhealthy tendencies and as he retreated further and further from his mother who seemed to him lost in drunken stupor, Kuri was left entirely to his own devices and his romantic imagination. He was indulged by the family but never given any direction. The marriage that was arranged for him outraged Kuri's romantic ideas as well as his sense of worth.

None of the proposals made for him had gone further than a few tentative negotiations, largely because of his mother's reputation and the scandal of his father's suicide. In that small village community nothing was ever forgotten, least of all anything to do with the Big House. Everything was stored in the collective memory and at the appropriate times brought out as a squirrel brings out a carefully harvested nut.

Why now, Kuri asked himself, had this lowly connection been made? He knew why and it fuelled his anger against his mother. If it were not for his mother he was sure they would long ago have found for him a girl not only beautiful, but from a family with good social standing as well as wealth. They did not understand that although he cared nothing for wealth, he who loved poetry, art and beauty, he could not be expected to ally himself with a nobody, the descendant of a servant. And that, if one did not mince matters with talk of a fabulously large dowry, jewellery, money for the renovation and upkeep of the Big House, was what his bride was.

His grandmother had soon discovered Maria Chedathi's identity. Having done so, she had wrestled with herself over the question of the alliance and had finally decided that for the sake of the house and the family it must go through. This decision once made, she never again openly referred to the bride's antecedents. No public reference was ever made (or permitted to be made) about the bride's grandmother's former lowly connection with the family. Perhaps, the old lady told herself, it was all to the good. The girl was young, much younger than Kuri, and would need to be kept in her place. Knowledge of her lowly antecedents would prevent her getting out of hand.

III

Young Maria

9

When young Maria was told of the marriage that had been arranged for her, her heart was full of dissent. What she could not understand was how her grandmother could consider an alliance with the family of the Big House where she had once been a menial, yet it quickly became apparent to her that it was an alliance both old Maria and her father very much desired.

Mathen, her father, had made money, lots and lots of it, but he did not in his own country, his village, have name or standing because his ancestors had been poor and lowly and he was judged by them. His father had been a paid employee and his mother a domestic servant; the one unremarkable, the other someone to be ashamed of. By marrying his daughter to a scion of the Big House, even if it had fallen on hard times, Mathen would give his daughter the place in society that had been denied to him and which he had always coveted. Marriage was not an individual affair, it affected the whole family. With his money and their name, his descendants, Maria's children, would be foremost in society. It was a heady feeling.

In the face of her father's dreams of the future and her grandmother's memories of the past, Maria's objections to the people of the Big House seemed self-centred and feeble. After all, why should she resent what her grandmother seemed not to? Why should she object to her father financing a ne'er do well family if he did not? She would have liked to make a love marriage and was fairly sure that if they had stayed on in Singapore she would have found someone for herself. However, when the return to Kerala had come about she had more or less accepted that her family would arrange her marriage. There was little or no scope for her to meet eligible young men. She also believed that, once married, she would be set free to lead the life she wanted. Many a young girl embraces matrimony with this idea in mind.

It was in the remoter corners of her mind that Maria stored away her dreams (and what were they but dreams?) of love, romance, glamour such as she had glimpsed in foreign films and read about in books. She also realized that she would have to come to terms with her childish dislike of the people of Big House, that she must cease to see them as oppressors. Young Maria was, essentially, an eminently sensible girl.

Nevertheless, Maria could not help but feel a little disturbed by the gloating note that had entered into her father and grandmother's voices when they spoke of the impending marriage. Often now, they reminisced together about the old days, of the humiliation, the hard work, the privation, they had known. "Do you remember," Mathen asked his mother and everything they said seemed to begin like that, "how the sons of the Big House beat up young Jose and when you rushed to rescue him the mistress said that servants had to be beaten?"

"Oh yes, that was when the old woman regained her speech," old Maria replied, nodding her head, "they thought they were above everybody, but now those same 'servants' are the ones to whom they have to look to maintain them."

This, with variations, was the theme of all the conversations between Maria's father and grandmother. Until the day when another note was struck. Mathen came back from a visit into town and asked his daughter to leave the room. Maria obeyed, but being only human, remained behind the door to listen.

"After all," she said to Bimbo, the big alsatian that accompanied her everywhere, "since I'm not supposed to hear, its bound to be about me. I may be old enough to be married but they still think they have to protect me. Whose life is it any way?" Hearing the question mark, Bimbo raised his face to answer with one of his all purpose barks that took care, in his opinion, of the many mystifying and boring things humans did and said such as standing motionless behind a door when so much more fun could be had by bounding in and knocking someone or something over. Maria, however, quickly shushed him; she needed silence to be able to eavesdrop effectively.

"Mother," she heard her father say, "I heard a disturbing story today. Rumour has it that Kuri's father committed suicide and that his mother is a drunk. Do you really think we should proceed with this marriage?"

"It is true," his mother replied, "that Baben, Kuri's father, committed suicide. But that was many years ago, over 30 years now if my memory serves me correctly. Baben was a weak boy, spoiled by his mother and then married to a wife who did not care for him and said many hurtful things to him. It is my belief she was too passionate for him and of course, she was very much younger..." the elder Maria's voice tailed off here because she had remembered that young Maria was also much younger than her husband to be. "Any way, to cut a long story short, to punish her and his mother for marrying him to her, Baben committed suicide. It was always my belief that he never really intended to die, that he expected to be found by someone, but it turned out otherwise. As for the mother, Kunjam, it is no wonder if she drinks. What else can she do? She has lived all these years with hatred and silence, the Mistress was not the kind who would ever forgive. Poor thing," and old Maria sighed gustily and enjoyably, "too young to be a widow and some might say too hot blooded."

"If you are sure that is all!" muttered Mathen. "Name or no name, family or no family, I would not give my little girl where there is such insanity. What of this alcoholic mother?"

"Alcoholism is not inherited, it is something that is learnt," old Maria said comfortably, "no, there is no need for you to worry on that score. Think instead of how much we are envied by all our friends, how our little girl is going to belong to one of the oldest families in this country. That is what we have to think about and praise God for."

"If you are sure," Mathen reiterated and "I am sure," responded his mother and the matter was closed. But not for young Maria. The idea of the suicide haunted her as much as the knowledge that she was to have a mother-in-law who drank. She wondered, as her father and grandmother had not, what kind of husband a man would be whose father had hanged himself before he was born and whose mother drank to escape the hatred that surrounded her. In a curious way, however, this intrigued her, she found it 'romantic' and it predisposed her to pity Kuri and pity, they say, is akin to love.

Mathen was busy making the financial arrangements that preceded the wedding. The unusually large dowry had to be paid in advance. Money for refurbishing the big House, for getting it ready for the wedding, had also been demanded in advance. Grandmother Maria was occupied with making new jewellery for the bride, with laying in provisions of coconuts, spices and rice, all of which had to be prepared and kept in readiness to sustain the relatives who came for the wedding, every one of whom congratulated her on her good fortune and took pride in an alliance which raised their status as well. Only those more distantly connected sounded a note of dissonance.

"Marrying above yourself can only lead to unhappiness,"

croaked an old cousin three times removed. "It is better for like to marry like."

"Yes," agreed one whose relationship was so tenuous as to be almost honorary, "after all, what happens if they do not treat the child well? They may remind her that her grandmother was only a maid servant, how then will she be mistress in the house where her grandmother served?"

"It won't be easy for her any way," put in yet another, "she is already a little 'madaama' with her Singapore ways and the Big House people are old fashioned, orthodox." Maria senior refused either to be angered or grieved. Preparing and then chewing her tobacco, she replied placidly: "Times change and people with them. We are no longer the people we were when I worked for the Big House. Now it is the Big House that is poor and they need our money. Little Maria will be mistress of the Big House because it is her money that will restore it, her children who will inherit it. Therefore, none will dare say anything to or about her."

Almost everybody agreed with her, although some shook their heads and muttered darkly. Young Maria herself wondered; would they really accept her, or would they try and taunt her with being her grandmother's descendant? 'Let them just try', she told herself, clenching her fist, 'I will soon show them who is mistress of the Big House. If any one of them says anything against my grandmother or my family they will find I am no humble servant girl bowing and scraping to them.'

She had seen her husband to be only once when, accompanied by an aunt and uncle, he had come to see her. Shc had looked eagerly at him and thought him good looking; he was fair skinned and wore his hair rather long so that he was in the habit of tossing it off his forehead in, she thought, a rather attractive way. Kuri thought it made him look Byronic and Byron was a poet he much admired. He had looked at her hardly at all and spoken very little, giving her little chance to ply him with the questions she longed to ask. Although the elders had sat apart from them, allowing them to get acquainted, Maria knew they were surreptitiously watching and listening and it had inhibited her from bringing up the subject of his father's suicide and his mother's drinking or even his attitude to her antecedents.

She had been indignant when the aunt had asked her to fetch an object from the bureau across the room because she knew the woman had no interest in the object, that it was only a ploy to see how she walked, to make sure there was nothing wrong with her limbs.

"It is the way," grandmother had said in her usual comfortable way when, afterwards, Maria complained of being humiliated. "Many people have daughters with some deformity but they still want to see them well married and so they will try and hide the limp or whatever and not tell of polio or other such illness." Maria thought of how her Singapore friends would have reacted but she did not pursue the subject. She wanted to take the impressions she had of the man she was so soon to marry, so many brush strokes in her memory, and try to make a composite picture of him.

She remembered a certain arrogance in his manner but thought this had been belied by the look in his eyes which had seemed gentle, even wistful. His manner had been curt, bordering on brusque, but had there not been a hint of shyness behind it? He had looked younger than his years; she knew he was considerably older than she. His hands were long and the fingers slender, well manicured. In fact, everything about him bore the marks of an almost fastidious grooming. She had only a limited knowledge of the world so the words 'effete' or `foppish' did not occur to her. Instead, she wondered if he was strong of both mind and body like her father and grandmother, both of them well able to face a world not of their making and find in it their own place.

The one thing that seriously upset her was that Kuri was afraid of dogs and a big dog like Bimbo reduced him almost to a jelly, a fact that did not improve his temper. Bimbo, large and playful, had not improved his chances. Quickly sensing that Kuri was afraid of him, Bimbo had decided to capitalise on this unique state of affairs, (normally, even the cats and chickens were not afraid of him). Growling and bristling he refused to allow Kuri near his mistress and barked every time Kuri's eyes met his. Since he also wagged his tail, to the great danger of the food laid out on low tables, Bimbo believed that he was conveying an essentially non-violent message. Sadly, Kuri did not interpret the message correctly and he was adamant that Bimbo could not accompany Maria to the Big House.

"We will look after him for you," Maria's father reassured her, "he will always be here for you when you come home." Maria was in tears but she sustained herself with the memory of Kuri's rare and beautiful smile and resisted the anger that rose in her at all that she was giving up. In her heart of hearts, however, she never forgave him for that first sacrifice she made of her beloved dog. It is the little things, the small resentments, things given up, that smoulder in a marriage, sometimes remaining safely banked and at other times, flaring up into a conflagration no one can explain.

10

Maria had grown up in Singapore where, after her mother's death, Mathen had settled his mother and his daughter while he conducted his business in the remoter areas of Malaya. However, Maria had grown up knowing all about India even though she seldom went there. She knew especially about the state from where her family came; like all expatriates, the elder Maria might have physically left the place of her birth, but her roots had remained undisturbed where they were. Kerala, young Maria knew, was a small state that slithered up the south west coast of India on a map that looked to her like a woman in a sari. Once inside their house, Singapore was left behind the front door and young Maria was back in the land of her grandmother's birth. Maria was to think later that this perhaps had taught her adaptability; but when she was irritated she felt that it might have made her schizophrenic.

Maria had studied in a coeducational college in Singapore and she had had boy friends. However, she had never taken any of them home because had she done so, all her activities would have become subject to her grandmother's supervision. Her friends often laughed at her for being as over protected as she was.

"You're like a baby la," said Rose, "can't do this and can't do that."

Only Su Lin from a traditional Chinese home, understood and sympathized. "They watch you every single minute," she said, "so afraid we are going to get into trouble and make our family ashamed and lose face." But she had advice for Maria: "You don't have to tell them everything you do. Yes, I'm going to the pictures; yes, with Rose and Su Lin. Unless they ask 'who else?' you don't have to say 'and our boy friends'. Saves trouble and worry," she smiled wickedly.

Maria took that advice to heart; she went to the pictures and to the coffee house with Jo who was her friend Paula's brother. Jo was Eurasian and that in itself would not have endeared him to Maria's father and grandmother. "It's not as though you are going to marry him la," protested Rose and again, it was only Chinese Su Lin who understood.

Maria's relationship with Jo was innocent and she was given little opportunity to make it anything else, supervised as she was by her grandmother and her serving women. It had remained at the level of a few kisses, declarations of undying love, spiced by occasional gifts and love letters (secreted away in the college locker). The relationship had been cooling when the move to India came but, although she was not heartbroken,

Maria retained a desire to take up romance where she had left off. She wanted her husband-to-be to fulfil the part of romantic lover even though, as the other half of an arranged marriage, he had not been cast in that role. Kuri did not oblige. His few letters to her (in reply to hers) were terse and unromantic; however, there was one saving grace: Kuri wrote poetry and like any writer (especially unpublished, surviving in a philistine atmosphere) was glad of an audience. Maria was showered with poems and although she understood little or nothing of their content, she assumed that they were love poems and read into them what she wished. She also convinced herself that Kuri was an intellectual, full of deep thoughts. And that, too, was romantic. She and her Singapore friends (with the exception of down to earth Rose) had decided that intellectual men were 'sexy'. Kuri liked her enthusiastic reception of his poems (no one in the Big House could be bothered with them) and she imagined the two of them were in love. All too often, love is based on mistaken premises and some never discover that this is so.

Letters and the accompanying poems were acceptable but for the young couple to go out together was not. Maria chafed at the restriction but since Kuri said and did nothing about it, there was little that she could achieve. "But what's the sense of it?"Maria cried to her grandmother and then before that lady could reply, she said: "No, don't tell me, 'it's not the way'!" and she mimicked her grandmother's voice. "How are we supposed to get to know each other then?"

"You are a cheeky little girl," the grandmother chided affectionately, "but you are right, it is not the way. I suppose it is for your own protection. If anything were to go wrong at the last minute you would be less hurt by it and no one could gossip about you. Any way, you have your letters. That's more than most girls got in the old days. Most girls never even saw their husbands before marriage."

Old Maria felt guilty because it had not been so for her. She had chosen her own husband and no one had tried to protect her good name. That was one of the few advantages of not belonging to the upper class. It was sad that it could not be the same for young Maria. "Well," she told herself in extenuation, "they will have a long time together and they will be happy." She did not recognize it as such, but old Maria had the habit of positive thinking. Exasperated, Maria stormed off to write another long and passionate letter to Kuri and to vent her annoyance in letters to her friends in Singapore who all responded by telling her variously that it was 'too cute', 'too funny la', 'too ridiculous for words'. When she received those letters, Maria was more annoyed than ever. For a while after her marriage Maria had maintained her links with her Singapore friends, but as the gulf between them widened and as her feelings became too complex for expression in letters, she allowed the friendship to lapse and this too, like the loss of Bimbo the dog, she resented and unconsciously laid the blame at Kuri's door.

She thought a great deal about sex as well during this time which seemed to her like a lull between her life as a young girl and the grown up world she was going to enter as a wife and in the fullness of time, a mother. Like most young girls on the brink of matrimony she wondered what it would be like to have breakfast with the same man for the next forty or fifty years. Would she be bored? Wouldn't he get tired of her before that? Everything that she had read suggested that sex was the most important thing in the world and yet in Pallisseri it seemed as if it were the last thing on anyone's mind. Young people did not go out together and young married couples remained rigidly separate when they were out together. It was hard to imagine any of those she met in the village doing those strange and erotic things she had read about. She tried in an oblique fashion to bring the subject up with her grandmother who assumed that Maria was asking for information, whereupon she proceeded to deliver a birds and bees type of lecture that was rudely nipped in the bud by her granddaughter who informed her indignantly that she had studied biology as well as physiology and knew the facts of life. "I know where babies come from and what makes them. Thank you very much," Maria said and stalked off. 'Then what did she want to know?' her puzzled grandmother asked herself. Perhaps young Maria did not know either. Secretly, old Maria was relieved; although she herself had enjoyed her sexual life with her husband, she could not have brought herself to speak of sex to her grandchild.

She was shackled by the taboos of her society that outlawed sex and relegated it to the dead of night. When people talk about marriage being a woman's destiny, they are not talking about sexual happiness although, perhaps unconsciously, they may consider the man's satisfaction.

Meanwhile, family and friends began to gather in the house in preparation for the wedding day. Maria found herself being examined closely by a bunch of old women who studied her features, her dress and paid special attention to her jewellery. None of them seemed to subscribe to the rule that it was rude to make personal remarks; they commented freely on her looks (some compared her unfavourably with her mother), disapproved of the way she spoke ('like a foreigner'), of the way she behaved ('too forward'), and with the exception of a very few, seemed to think that she had got the best of the bargain in marrying into the Big House.

"Why?" demanded Maria of one old crone, "the Big House is just a house and not in a very good condition, judging by the money my father is handing over for its repair. So why not say they are lucky?"

"Aiyo!" exclaimed the women, "she knows nothing. Big House is one of the oldest family names in this district. They have been rich landowners for countless generations, they are aristocrats."

Despite herself, Maria felt a thrill to hear this. Ever since she could remember she had had money; position and the prestige that goes with it, however, had been denied to her. Nevertheless, she did not give in easily: "My father can buy and sell them, aristocrats or no," she said loftily and then felt ashamed of herself.

The *kalyana orappu* was held: a formal and restrictive function, from which both bride and groom were excluded, at which the elders from both families met to decide the date of marriage, dowry, ornaments, number of guests; this dialogue was held between paternal relatives only.

The *orappu* was followed by the *virunnu*, a formal feast at which the dowry changed hands, and symbolic of the entry of the daughter-in-law, *marumakkal*, the head of the girl's house, her father, stood on a mat in centre of room, elbows crossed horizontally, *kavani* tied at waist. All the important details connected with the forthcoming wedding were announced: whose children were about to be united, the date and hour of marriage, the *thoka* given as dowry, of which, traditionally, forty per cent went to the church.

A prayer was then said by the parish priest after which the two *karanavans* or heads of the two households embraced each other, Kuri's uncle and Maria's father.

The ceremony concluded with the lighting of *kole vilakku,* oil lamps, by a female relative of the bride.

The last step in the elaborate list of rituals was the inviting of guests. Each person had to be personally invited, asked to participate: *kalyanam koodanam.* A male and a female member of the household, one of whom had to be of mature years, went from house to house to extend the invitation.

Nadda varkam, the second step by which the bride joins the husband's sabha was performed and again, a percentage of the dowry was given to the church.

A month before the wedding, hectic preparation of food had begun; coconuts, spices, rice were prepared and packed away, while negotiations were begun for the purchase of whole fish, poultry and meat.

Meanwhile, the *thattan* or family jeweller was busy making the *thali* and other gold ornaments. The *pannen* (tailor), *asari* (carpenter) and others associated with preparing the wedding trappings come to the house the day before the wedding. The *thattan* placed the *minnu* in a small shallow bronze vessel containing rice, a symbol of fertility. The *minnu* is a small fleck of gold ornamented by a cross, made of 7 or 14 tiny gold beads. The *thattan* was then paid in cash and given betel leaves and areca, symbolizing a relationship that is not merely commercial. All the servicing castes: blacksmith, carpenter, barber, tailor and washerwoman were given a measure of rice known as *edangari,* raw bananas, oil, coconut, and a *dakshina* or ceremonial fee.

The rituals of bathing and ornamentation on the night before the wedding are very important and the female relatives were all agog. There was a great deal of excitement and *korava villikuga*, hooting, accompanied the ceremonial bathing.

The barber and a washerwoman are in charge of groom and bride in their respective houses. These traditional attendants were given gifts of food, clothes and a bowl of *pachor* or sweet rice.

On the night before the wedding, the groom's sister's husband has to remove seven threads from the *mantrakodi,* the bridal sari or cloth given to the bride, in order to fashion a string for the marriage *minnu* to be put around her neck. The seven threads are twisted into a single thread on which to hang the *minnu.* This is followed by a *suddhi* (feast) for kinsfolk, neighbours and the servicing castes, all fed ceremonially but separately. As Kuri had no sister, a cousin's husband was pressed into service.

In this fashion the two young people (and one of them was not so young) prepared for matrimony; with half hopes, resentments, ignorance and in Maria's case, a kind of courage, because she sensed (if she did not know) that she was entering mined territory that she would never leave until her death.

11

By mutual consent it had been left to Kuri to inform Kunjam, his mother, of the marriage that had been arranged for him. He waited for her to comment sarcastically on the fact that his bride was the granddaughter of an erstwhile servant, the cook Maria Chedathi.

As usual, Kunjam did not do what was expected of her. Because almost no one in the family had very much to do with her, they did not know the ways in which Kunjam had changed from the bitter young woman who had been first Baben's wife and then his widow. For many years, while Kuri was growing up, she had been an embarrassment for the family because of her drinking, someone to be hustled out of sight and kept away from visitors to the house. Slowly, it had become second nature to treat her as if she did not really exist.

Kunjam was bitter, indeed. As she was to tell Maria later: "I was so filled up with bitterness that I choked on it like bile rising into one's mouth." But, as the years passed, she had begun to think about her life and the disaster that had overtaken her and her husband. She had pondered deeply on the reasons for Baben's suicide and she had come face to face with the truth. She had forced herself to consider the part she had played in his drama and she had convinced herself that, although perhaps not blameless, her tragedy was that of being the wrong person in the wrong place.

"It was," she tried to tell her own family, on her infrequent visits to them, "Baben who was always at fault. He did not have courage to live and be what he wanted so he preferred to die. I might have felt sorry for him, but he never loved me and he did not allow me to love him or pity him. He thought only of himself but he never gave a thought to what would happen to me and for that I shall never forgive him. For the way his family have behaved to me I shall never forgive them either."

Her visits home to her family grew more infrequent with the years for she quickly realised that they were uncomfortable with her bitterness and were ashamed of her and the truths she tried to reveal to them. Had her marriage been successful, even if not happy, they would have welcomed her as a daughter to be proud of, a daughter married into the Big House family. As a daughter so patently a failure, they did not want to know her or to hear of her troubles and so, after her mother's death, Kunjam almost entirely ceased her visits to her childhood home.

Now Kuri stood before her and told her that he was soon to be married. That he was not overjoyed at the prospect, she could see.

"Son," Kunjam said to him, "do not marry if you do not want to. An unhappy marriage is not unhappy for one person only, two people are made miserable and although you may not believe me, it is the woman who suffers the more, perhaps because she has so much less of her own any way. Have the courage to stand up to your grandmother and say you will not marry, if that is what you feel."

"Mother, it is all arranged and it is my duty. She is a rich girl and it is what this house, this family, need." Kuri avoided his mother's eyes as he spoke.

"Then may God help her, may God give the poor girl the strength to live a life of disappointment," Kunjam broke out, her voice quivering. She saw the look of distaste that crossed her son's face and knew that, as usual, he was ashamed of her, of her emotion, of everything she stood for. She went closer to her son and before he could resist, she took his face in her hands and forced him to look at her.

"Son," she said, "I have not drunk today, not yet. For just a little while, try to treat me as your mother. I have done no wrong and yet you and your grandmother treat me like a criminal. Should I have died, killed myself like your father? Is that what you wanted too? Would you then have treated me as a saint? Is it flesh and blood that you cannot stand?"

She turned away and left him and Kuri went straight to his room where he sat and tried to come to terms with what he saw as his unfortunate life, saddled with an impossible mother and now with a wife whom he himself would never have chosen.

Kunjam too, went to her room and paced up and down like a caged animal. Her faithful maid Katri poured out a glass of the ubiquitous 'medicine' for her and Kunjam reached for it eagerly. "They are getting Kuri married," she told the maid, "they are marrying him to that Maria Chedathi's grandchild."

"Yes, I know, I was going to tell you," replied Katri. "It seems the family did very well in foreign parts and that Maria Chedathi is now a very wealthy woman."

"Wealthy enough to buy Kuri for the child," and Kunjam began to laugh. "Does she not understand that nobody here wants the girl, only her money? I wish I could meet the child, what is her name? Oh yes, Maria... I would warn her that this marriage could never bring her happiness. Does she not want to be happy?"

Katri was experienced enough to see that the 'medicine' was having its effect. "You must not worry," she said soothingly, "it will be different for her maybe. They say she has lived in Singapore or some such place and she will know much better how to manage than you did, today's girls are different anyway. And Kuri is different too. He will not..." the maid's voice tailed away.

Kunjam laughed and it was not a pleasant sound. "Not hang himself like his father? No, perhaps not, but will it be she who is driven to hang herself? Hate nourishes some people, but not all... If only I could see her..."

The maid knew, only too well, that the family would never permit this. She had orders to bundle her mistress out of sight of visitors and strangers, to keep up the deception about the ailing daughter-in-law.

So, while the house was being readied for the impending marriage, Kunjam was kept largely in the dark about the events that were taking place. Kuri did not visit his mother to tell her of his meeting with his bride, nor did he inform her of Maria's frequent, enthusiastic letters to him and he certainly never told his mother of the poems he copied out and sent to Maria.

What no one suspected was Kunjam's passionate interest in her daughter-in-law to be. Kunjam vowed to herself that she would befriend the girl as her mother-in-law had never befriended her. So strong was her intention that for many weeks before the wedding she abstained from drinking and despite the agonies this caused her, she was determined to stay sober so as not to be misjudged by the young bride when she came to Big House for the first time.

When, in fact, young Maria arrived Kunjam did not find her intention so easy to carry through. Maria looked at her with disapproval and sought never to be alone with Kunjam who was reduced to following the girl about from room to room. Long years of virtual isolation had rendered Kunjam rusty in the arts of socialising and she could not easily find words that would win the girl over to her. But she would not give up.

Kunjam noticed that no one was particularly friendly with the newcomer in their midst. She noticed, too, that Maria hung back from intimacy with Kuri's beloved grandmother. That, of course, pleased her greatly.

She watched as Maria set about doing up the old house, immersing herself in the repairs and the new construction. She wanted to tell the girl that it was not enough, could never be enough, but she could not find the words. And when the words came, they were the wrong words, they came out wrong, not what she had intended to say at all and she could have wept with frustration.

"A house for a husband?" she had asked and although it sounded mocking that was not the way she had intended it.

To her surprise, however, Maria had turned and asked her, albeit haughtily, what she meant and although, again, she was unable to explain exactly what she meant, it quickly became apparent to her that Maria was interested.

Maria was also lonely and now, recognising an ally, it was to her mother-in-law that she turned and to whom increasingly she would turn as time went on. Gradually, she would build up a relationship with Kuri's grandmother but it was to Kunjam whom she would grow close.

12

The day of the wedding dawned at last and Maria was made ready for the journey to the church in Veloorkada. It was a Sunday because that was the day on which Christ rose from the dead and *rahukaalam*, the inauspicious time of Saturn, was expected to be over early. Maria's departure from the natal church was symbolised by a letter or *desa kuri* which stated that there were no dues owing, that the bride had not been excommunicated and so on.

The priest had come and facing east, he had prayed for all in the house. Maria had gone through the ritual of *guru dakshina* in which she had presented a sum of money wrapped in betel leaves to her first teacher. As she had never been to school in Pallisseri, she had made the presentation to an old man who had taught her father and his brothers in the village school so long ago. Kuri, in the Big House, had made a similar presentation to his first teacher. This was a part of the rituals of separation, the *yatra chothikkal,* when all the senior relatives are called upon for their blessing. Maria's elderly relatives had crowded round, placing wet and noisy kisses on her cheeks.

Maria had taken a tearful farewell of Bimbo who had licked her wet face and looked at her with eyes that surely accused her of betrayal. "I can't help it, Bimbo," she assured him, "Kuri is afraid of you, but one of these days I promise you I'll be back to get you." She had then got ready and climbed into the car that was to convey them to Veloorkada, closing her ears to Bimbo's howls and barks as he was confined in a room to prevent him from trying to run behind the car, something he had done before.

In the car with her were her grandmother and the girl cousin who would stand behind her during the ceremony until her husband's family took over.

The car was in the porch and all the occupants were seated in it but still it did not depart. "What are we waiting for?" Maria asked flippantly, "time we were off."

Her grandmother smiled: "In such a hurry to get married, little one? You should be crying and holding back, not urging us to go quickly! We are waiting for our cousins to arrive. They are your grandfather's closest relatives."

Just then Maria's father bustled up looking very serious. He said to his mother:

"There is bad news. It seems cousin Chella who was bitten by her cat developed rabies and she died early this morning. No one from that family can attend the wedding but we must delay the departure a little because we are now still in *rahukaalam*."

"Oh, for goodness sake!" Young Maria exploded, preparing to get out of the car. "It's boiling hot here, I'm going to sit inside the house."

"Stay where you are," her grandmother ordered, an unusual note in her voice. "You cannot go back inside the house now."

"Why not?" demanded the bride.

The elder Maria clearly hesitated between 'because I say so' and the real reason and wisely decided for the latter, because by the glint in her granddaughter's eye she knew that Maria would storm out of the car. "Because it is very unlucky to go back," she explained, "as it is..." her voice tailed off.

"As it is," Maria echoed defiantly, "it's a bad omen, isn't it? Well, I don't believe in all that stuff. The only bad omen as far as I am concerned is leaving Bimbo behind. Let's go, I say."

"Just ten minutes," her father pleaded and Maria, after a moment's pause, nodded imperiously. She felt defiant and suddenly angry but was relieved at being able to give in. She seized a fan offered by a cousin and looking away, began to fan herself vigorously, tears stinging her eyes. Why had cousin Chella died just then? Of all the unlucky things, to be bitten by one's own pet cat! Maria was angry because she was afraid, sensing that she needed all the luck in the world just then, not unlucky omens right at the start. She could hear Bimbo howling inside.

At last the signal was given, the inauspicious time had passed, and the cars moved off, travelling as fast as was safe on that narrow road with its variegated forms of traffic.

On approaching the church, she saw knots of people gathered outside waiting for the bridal car. Kuri then entered by the western door and was seated on the left of the aisle, facing the altar. Until he was in place the bride could not enter the church. In the marriage ceremony she played the passive role; as Maria had pointed out to her grandmother, who had not been impressed, she was the one who was being married, *kettichu vidunna pennu* and not the one who married, *kettunnavan*.

Of course, they were very late and the first thing Maria registered was the frown on her bridegroom's face as he waited for her. As in a blur she saw countless palmetto fans waving in the hot and airless church as an impatient congregation tried to keep cool.

Much of the marriage service was also a blur to her, mainly because it was in Syriac, the language of the orthodox Syrian Church. Later she joked and said that she could not be held to any of the promises she had made, as she had no idea what they were. She had meant it as a joke and was disconcerted to find that nobody seemed to think it funny at all. She saw her grandmother frown at her and could almost imagine that she had spoken: "Mind now, remember you are a married woman, not a spoilt little girl at home." It made young Maria suddenly realize that everything was irrevocably changed and for a moment she was afraid. Then she squared her shoulders, lifted her chin and made a face at her grandmother.

Maria had been to many weddings in Singapore where the church had always been beautifully decorated, with flowers everywhere: sprays of orchids, lilies like trumpets to announce the joyful event. The old church in Veloorkada was shabby and dark and little or no attempt had been made to spruce it up for the wedding. In no way did it resemble Singapore's grand St Andrew's Cathedral. Unlike the churches in Singapore, there was no organ or piano. The singing and the chanting of the Jacobite liturgy was led by the priests. It was straggly and unmelodious. Kuri and she stood at a table placed before the altar. It was covered with a pink tablecloth featuring improbable looking green and black parrots. Several priests stood at the altar; because of the importance of the Big House there were two Bishops in attendance.

Maria wondered what Kuri was thinking as he stood there beside her with the priests droning on incomprehensibly in front of them. It is a good thing that we cannot read each other's thoughts. Women love occasions and they revel in their thoughts, so many of them, flashing through their minds, deep and dark, rarely too deep for tears. Kuri was thinking of yesterday when he had been free; he longed for these tiresome ceremonies to be over, to be able to go back to his life, to his writing. Would life ever be the same again? He sighed; he supposed not. Maria heard the sigh and tears sprang to her eyes in sympathy. Kuri suppressed a yawn as the priests genuflected.

When the time came for the groom to tie the *minnu*, the little gold cross shaped like a grain of rice, around the bride's neck, it slipped from the priest's hand as he handed it to Kuri. A gasp of horror rose from the congregation because everyone knew that this was a very bad omen indeed. Then there was a collective sigh of relief as it was seen that Maria had caught at the thread and saved the *minnu* from falling to the floor. She handed it back to Kuri who tied it securely around her neck. Maria felt his hands shake as he tied the knot.

Kuri's grandmother asked what had happened and was told about Maria rescuing the *minnu*. "I see," remarked the old lady, "that the girl has presence of mind. Perhaps, after all, we are getting more than a good dowry." The women in the congregation commented that it was indubitably a bad omen and acting to avert it meant that Maria would have a hard time of it. Meaning the marriage would always be her responsibility. "Well, what else?" one of them queried, "in the end it all falls to the woman, that is what it is all about."

The *mantrakodi* was draped over Maria's head indicating that she had now left her family to join her husband's. Accordingly, her cousin stepped back and one of Kuri's female cousins (since he had no sister) took her place. It was an emotional moment and as if sensing the tears gathering in her eyes, Kuri turned and smiled at Maria. He had an attractive smile, all the more so for being rare and Maria really and truly fell in love with him at that moment. His poems (or what she had made of them) had predisposed her to love him but it was the smile at that particular moment that clinched it. All through the difficult years that lay ahead Maria never lost her sense of that moment.

As the bridal pair emerged from the church there was a sudden unheralded downpour of rain through which the sun continued to shine. "A jackal is getting married," said some, referring to the simultaneous sun and rain. "A very good omen," everyone opined.

Old Maria remembered then all the good omens there had been at her wedding so long ago; there had been the sudden shower of rain, on the way to the church a woman carrying pots filled to brimming with water and there had been a bangle seller. Yet Eapen had not lived long although the marriage had been happy. She sighed gustily, remembering, as did all the other women there. Their menfolk relaxed visibly, relieved that the long and boring service was over at last, leaving them free to smoke, to eat and to drink. The young ones secretly dreamed of the wedding days to come, the promise of unknown things. After the wedding ceremony it was strange for the elder Maria to enter the Big House as a guest, the grandmother of the bride. The house still looked strangely familiar. Although everything about her life since she was last there had changed completely, it seemed as if the Big House had remained the same. Everything was the same and yet the grandeur and the opulence that she remembered from her youth were there no more. Was it because she had changed, had seen other and better days? Despite the sprucing up for the wedding that the house had been subjected to, it looked shabby and run down and it depressed her to find it so.

She and the mistress of Big House confronted each other over the passage of years that had turned them both into old women, equals at least in that. There were perhaps not so many years between them but life had been hard to both of them in different ways and had laid its imprint on them. "Well," said Kuri's grandmother, "times have changed, have they not?"

"They have indeed. God has been good to me and mine," Maria replied sanctimoniously, gaining courage from the thought that it was their money, her son's money, that from now on would keep the Big House. "God be praised," she added.

The other woman's rejoinder was not without malice: "Let us hope that your grandchild is as good a cook as you were, whatever else she may have learned elsewhere."

The elder Maria's face darkened but she answered placidly enough: "Oh, she knows everything she needs to know, there are no good-for-nothings in my family."

Having crossed swords and tested each other's mettle, the two women resumed the parts they had to play that day: two equals whose descendants had been united in marriage. Each saw in the other the changes that time and circumstance had wrought and it caused a lessening of tension between them.

For the young Maria, too, entering the Big House was a strange experience. She had heard it described a hundred times by her grandmother and it had represented in her young mind many things: a place of grandeur, of shining floors, gabled roofs such as she had known in old Singapore and rich age-dark carvings on walls and lintels, a cruel place of injustice and inequality, a house full of lordly people, wondrous in some kind of way as they had been to Maria the servant girl. The house did not live up to her grandmother's descriptions of it. The young Maria had visualized the Big House as a magical place not far removed from a palace; instead she saw a sprawling house, comfortless and old fashioned, dark and warren like. As she approached it with her new husband who took her right hand in his and they both stepped over the threshold, right foot first, it seemed to have a darkly brooding air, hunched up, seeming to lie in wait. She shook off the fancy and as the sun came out from behind a temporary rain cloud and lit the house in a golden sheen, Maria noticed the carved wooden posts and lintels, the dark and massive rafters, the black and shining floor. Unbeknown to her, the house was beginning to cast its spell upon her.

As was the custom of *Ammae epichu*, literally giving to his mother, Kuri took his bride first to where Kunjam was standing a little apart from the family, with only her faithful maid beside her. Kunjam looked eagerly into the girl's face and then tentatively, tenderly, put out a hand and caressed Maria's cheek.

A cousin's wife stepped forward to offer the bridal couple a cup of milk, which is a symbol of fertility. Another cousin followed, holding a miniature *kindi,* a spouted vessel containing water, a lit *kole vilakku* (oil lamp), a *kinni* or shallow container which held a betel leaf, water, a fine muslin cloth with powdered rice and a few grains of unhusked rice in it. A small hole was then made in the cloth, while the cousin, head covered by her gold bordered *kavani*, faced the couple who turned to the east, associated with Jesus and the rising sun. She then dipped the muslin containing the rice into the water and touched it first to Kuri's and then Maria's brow three times. The spouted vessel was the symbol of masculinity, while the shallow *kinni* was feminine; the unhusked rice grains stood for reproduction and the powdered rice signified consummation. Fortunately, Maria was too busy concentrating to think about the symbolism or she might have burst into a fit of giggles.

There were rituals about eating as well. The lunch was prefaced by the priest asking: "Have all arrived?" Then, after assent, "Have all sat?" If this is not done, her grandmother had explained to Maria, serious quarrels could (and very often did) erupt. "Etiquette is very important," she emphasised, "there is a good reason for all these customs and we must observe them."

At the end of the feast, the priest asks: "Have all eaten?"

Each person then sat with fists closed (*kai madakkuka*) and waited till all had finished. The departing guests were then sprinkled with rosewater, given lime, flowers, sandalwood paste and areca nuts and betel leaves.

Then followed the ritual gift exchange: Maria's mother's brother was the first recipient; for some obscure reason he is expected to tie a turban on his head and jeer and hoot. He received a gift of cloth and in return placed a gold ring on Kuri's finger. Then it was the bride's mother, paternal and maternal grandmothers' turn to receive gifts of cloth and give gold rings in exchange. Two aunts stood in for Maria's dead mother and maternal grandmother.

The wedding feast had been laid out in the front rooms and the bridal pair had been placed in front of the portrait of Baben in the living room. Now, as all the ceremonies were concluded, she turned to him and asked:

"Is that your father?"

"Yes," the answer was short, "he died before I was born. I never knew him."

It was said in such a way as to preclude the response that Maria wanted to make. Implicit in the terseness of Kuri's reply was the fact that it was not a subject he wanted to pursue. Maria felt rebuffed. She was on the brink of a relationship that she wanted, hoped would be the closest she would ever have with anybody in the world; one in which there would be no secrets, no holding back. Yet, already she saw the blank spaces, the distances that come to people later in their lives. She glimpsed them, a lonely vista, in Kuri's remote eyes. Would he always seek to escape her searching or would they find one another and discover themselves as she had read people in love did? There was so little she knew about men, about living together, but she was very ready to learn.

She was reminded of her grandmother's words: "In the beginning there should be hope, at the end there should be contentment." Well, she was hopeful, she was brim full of hope.

13

The first few months after their marriage were a time of testing, in which the young couple assessed each other, tried to discover the people they had created in their minds, charted by letters and poetry. They very soon discovered, however, that they were in uncharted territory, strangers to one another. Kuri seemed to remember little or nothing of Maria's outpourings in her letters and she, in her turn, realized that Kuri's poems had cast no dazzling light over his character. She found that instead of entering into his mind, she had read into his poetry what she had wanted and needed.

Kuri was very much older than she. Although this ought to have made her look up to him the more, Maria found him curiously immature in many ways and in others his age seemed to make him sedate and therefore, although she was loath to admit it, almost boring. Kuri did not like to lose face, he needed to be right always; he had, however unconsciously, a belief in male superiority. This meant that he was unwilling to try new things, to make mistakes and to laugh at himself, characteristics that make people seem older than they are.

Sex, the unknown and tantalising, had been satisfying enough, they were both young and healthy, but both of them had expected great things, had looked to sex as a magic casement that would open on to a wondrous new world, revealing them to each other, mentally and physically uniting them as nothing else can. This had not happened. Their physical intimacy did not lead to anything further, except perhaps to a sense of belonging, the ease of familiarity.

Despite his age, Kuri was largely inexperienced and very touchy about it. As both boy and young man he had grown up among male friends whose reactions to everything sexual in their adolescent world had consisted of sniggers and when very excited, shrill whistles and catcalls. Kuri had not always wished to participate in this way but he had a great need to belong with his peer group, had never wished in any way to be singled out as peculiar or different from the others. He had always kept his poetry secret from his boyhood friends. He was a follower, not a leader. Yet a part of him wanted to be different, daring, innovative and passionate and when he found himself only humdrum, he resented it. It was natural that he should blame Maria; it was her fault that she did not inspire him, did not raise him to the heights that he believed his poetic nature aspired to.

When Maria declared: "I want to be loved, I want to know love, to feel it," Kuri felt an urge to respond but could not. He had never known the kind of love Maria wanted, had never seen it. His father, clearly, had never loved his mother in that way and he had long ago realized that his mother embodied bitterness and frustration. He had never known his grandmother as anything but the Mistress of Big House, an old woman with cares and concerns that were far removed from the romantic. His uncles and aunts were all greying practitioners of the art of love, not given to any public or overt demonstrations, even of conjugal affection. There was nothing to be learned from them except restraint, the avoidance of physical expression. Kuri had never seen (and did not expect to see) anyone kissing in public. Only young people of the same sex held hands or embraced in public. Male and female, they led their separate lives. His own sexual experience had been limited to fumbling about with a prostitute in the nearby town and then the lonely masturbation. So Kuri turned away from Maria and brusquely told her not to be silly.

Maria, too, had no real experience of love between man and woman. Her grandmother spoke much about her departed husband, but if there had ever been passion there it could not be discerned in her comfortable references to the past. Maria had never really known her mother who had been an invalid for a long while before her early death and though her father, too, spoke of his dead wife with affection, it was always her goodness that he extolled and he had remained steadfast in his refusal to remarry and this, Maria thought, could be interpreted as stemming from a dislike of marriage and all that it involved.

Her own tentative dealings with Jo in Singapore, she was wise enough to realize, were no blueprint for her future with her husband. However, with Jo she had glimpsed something that she now wanted to extend and could not. She was careful never to refer to any of the boys she had known in Singapore. Somehow she knew that only trouble lay that way; she was a virgin but she also had to act virginal because husbands such as Kuri demanded that their wives should have no past.

Maria missed her carefree life in Singapore, her shopping expeditions with her friends to Orchard Road, visits to the cinema, outings of all sorts. In the Big House, people sometimes came to call and the neighbours invited the newly weds on a round of traditional dinners, but there was little or no social life.

Maria needed to be up and doing. So she turned her attention to the house. Traditional, with its tiled and gabled roof, it was quaint, it was old fashioned, it was inconvenient, but it was undoubtedly beautiful. It was also unusual in a world that seemed inexorably intent on throwing away the traditional and replacing it with glass and concrete.

She put her money to use, restoring the beautiful carved and wood-panelled walls, the exquisite black floor, the heavy wooden doors, comfortable seating on the wide verandas that gave on to the central courtyard. Ruthlessly, however, she set about demolishing the dark kitchen, put in modern bathrooms to replace the old room where the family squatted before huge copper urns filled with water and shiny spouted utensils of bell metal, the floors slick with generations of oil baths; and she replaced the outdoor toilet with modern water closets. Maria was terrified of snakes and had squatted in the outdoor lavatory reluctantly, constantly listening for suspicious rustling and movement in the matting lean-to.

Workmen filled the house and the sound of hammering and drilling almost drowned out the non-stop shrilling of the cicadas outside. The family watched and said nothing. Always Maria was aware of eyes that watched her every move. Few made any attempt to approach her and none showed any overt interest in her plans and Kuri, when she asked him what he thought, only replied: "It was well enough before, but when we grow used to the greater convenience I am sure we will all be happy and grateful to you."

She was aware of his sarcasm and resented it, but when she taxed him with it, he denied all such intention: "You read too much into what I say. If it makes you happy, knock the whole thing down and build again," saying which, Kuri returned to his reading and Maria stormed away to issue directions to the workmen.

She had not had much to do with Kuri's mother, Kunjam, but it had not taken her very long to divine the contents of a brown bottle that both Kunjam and her faithful maid described as medicine, a nerve tonic. With the moral rectitude of the very young, she disapproved of drinking and tended to avoid her mother-in-law. But Kunjam seemed almost to dog her footsteps and wherever Maria went, she soon found Kunjam not far behind, always offering conversation.

Now it was Kunjam who put into words what everybody understood and most people did not want to hear: "A house for a husband," she said mockingly, watching Maria direct the workmen.

"I don't know what you mean," Maria replied haughtily, not looking up from her tape measure.

"Everyone has to have something in this life, something to live for," Kunjam responded, "for you perhaps, it will be this house. Why not? Wood and cement can be satisfying enough. Perhaps you are wise. I have neither house nor husband, I am unwanted, but I can see that you have more sense than me, you won't go my way."

Maria looked at Kunjam then with new interest. Bored and unable to find any other companionship in Big House, she gradually began to gravitate towards Kuri's mother whom she found unafraid of anything, spirited, although well acquainted with pain. That she was also well acquainted with spirit of another kind, the contents of the bottle that never left her side, Maria had discovered soon enough and had disapproved, but now she decided to overlook it.

"Never let them see you cry," Kunjam said to Maria one day, catching her unawares and in tears, "look up and laugh!"

She shook her fist at the sky and with her face upturned it was hard to tell whether she meant the gods above or the family of the Big House. "I laugh, I look up and I laugh and laugh. There is no other way for women. I know, for I have cried a river in which I could have drowned. They tried to stop my drinking, my secret medicine, but I would rather drown in that than in salty tears." She flourished her bottle and for a brief while her laugh was mirthful. Maria joined in.

Maria knew that the rest of the family disapproved of Kunjam and, therefore, of her growing intimacy with her. It made her feel conspiratorial, almost like getting her own back on the family for all the humiliation suffered by her grandmother in days gone by. She quickly learned that there was no love lost between Kuri's mother and his grandmother and it pleased her that her friendship with Kunjam displeased the older woman whom at first she perceived as the enemy. Besides, she genuinely enjoyed her mother-in-law's company.

Kuri, on the other hand, had never been close to his mother, not since her outburst against his father long ago. He was uncomfortable then and it had been easy to move away from her, to align himself with his grandmother who, although powerful, never took away from him his sense of his own importance. His mother unmanned him and she embarrassed him. She did not think or speak as other people did.

One day Maria plucked up the courage to ask Kunjam why she drank. "I had seen other people, men, gain oblivion. It had that effect on me and that was what I wanted. To escape. Why do you think they don't want women to drink? Because we can escape that way, out of their clutches, away from our miseries and the narrow space they allow us. When we drink we begin to express ourselves, to say things that they do not want to hear; our voices rise, are no longer soft and charming; our faces contort and are no longer smoothly pleasing. We lose our dignity, begin to behave in ways they have told us are not good ways for women because they frighten men."

"But isn't it true?" Maria asked, "we shouldn't lose our inhibitions, should we? At least," she added doubtfully, "that is what they always tell us."

"They, they, they!" exclaimed Kunjam. "They tell us to do something and we must. Why? I ask why now and it is too late. I should have asked it not once but a hundred times when I was young, when I was your age. But I did not. I did as 'they' told me and look where it has landed me." She took a long convulsive swallow from the bottle in her hand and after a few moments she seemed to regain control of herself.

"They don't like us to drink because women, 'they' say, must always be dignified, how else, 'they' ask, can they respect and cherish us? We must be good. As long as women keep their dignity, their reserve, men can go on misbehaving. It is a man's world, child, and that's the way they want to keep it." Kunjam drank from the bottle and stared out at the blaze of green and golden afternoon. Everyone else was asleep after the midday meal.

"I had a sister once," she said, "she was much older than I and she was very beautiful. People in families like mine believe that it is so easy for a girl to lose her good name, especially if she is beautiful. If men look at a girl lasciviously, in some way it is her fault. So they married her off when she was ten. The boy, for that was what he was, was not normal, not quite right in the head. He was not violent or bad, in fact he was an affectionate boy who loved my sister very much. But he remained a little boy and the ten-year-old girl grew up. They had their first child before she was twelve and my sister treated the baby like a doll; one day she tried to clean her in the river and the baby nearly drowned. Her husband stood by and laughed because he thought it was a game. That was when my sister knew she had more than one child, that she had married one."

"What happened?" Maria asked.

"Nothing," Kunjam replied, "she did not hang herself, she got on with her life and if she found some way around the tragedy of being married to a child-man, she never let anybody guess it, but none of the children she had later looked like her husband!" Kunjam smiled mischievously.

Kuri steadfastly refused to talk about his father's suicide, but Maria found that his mother was willing to talk about anything, released at last by Maria's companionship from years of hurtful silence.

"Baben," said Kunjam, imbibing freely from what she

consistently alluded to as her medicine bottle, although she did not falsify its contents, "did not hang himself from that old breadfruit tree for love of some unattainable woman as everyone thought. At first, for ever such a long time, I thought so too; thought, as I'm sure his mother did also, that the woman was your grandmother Maria Chedathi. She was older than him but very good looking and knew it, was never one to hang back and many men lust after servant girls, so there was good reason to think it was she. But the truth, I think, was much worse and he could not face it and that is why he took his own life. Had it been your grandmother, he could have had her one way or another, his mother would have denied him nothing..."

"You talk as if my grandmother was some toy that anyone could play with, break as they like," Maria interrupted angrily, all her old defences up. She hated to see her beloved grandmother through the eyes of the Big House family.

"That's the way it was," answered Kunjam indifferently, "our sort of people didn't give a toss about that class of person."

"What class of person?" anger boiled over, "she was a human being, wasn't she, just like the rest of you and as it turned out, with more character than any of you in this so called Big House."

Kunjam drank again from the bottle and her eyes were becoming heavy. "Yes," she muttered, "that is why the old woman hated her so much. She was only a servant but she was worth far more than any of us, especially me. A woman like her could have been the making of Baben, practical and independent; but his mother could not arrange such a marriage. Like has to marry like. In any case, as I found out later, it was not her he wanted and it was not me either. He painted pictures of women but even those he changed, as I discovered later." Her voice was becoming slurred, her eyes heavy.

"What do you mean?" Maria asked curiously, "changed how?"

She was answered by a gentle snore and turned away in disgust just as Kunjam opened an eye and said: "The old woman knows. I don't know when she found out the truth, but I swear she knows it now. Why don't you ask her the next time you go in there to massage her legs? Yes, I've seen you, good little wife and daughter-in-law!" Then she laughed maliciously, "Your grandmother was lucky, for she was no better than she should be. She thought Baben fancied her, always flaunting herself in front of him, even though she was older, even after she was married. But she was lucky..." Kunjam turned on her side and shut her eyes, but not before Maria had seen the tears.

Sometimes she wondered what really had taken place all those years ago. What was the secret that Kunjam hinted at, always retreating from it at the last moment? It was also hard for Maria to imagine her staid, pragmatic old grandmother as a flirtatious girl and she wished sometimes that she could turn the years backwards and be able to look down the tunnel of time. It all added to the fascination of Big House.

14

Maria was ever conscious of her husband's cousin Rachie because, it seemed to her, that wherever she turned, Rachie somehow was there, either furtively watching or boldly staring. She was not friendly. When challenged, Rachie tossed her head and answered haughtily: "I can look at anyone if I want to. This is my house too, you know and I have the right to be anywhere I like, do whatever I wish."

"You are not free to spy on me," retorted Maria, "nor to follow me around always watching and listening."

"Listen to the madama," Rachie taunted her, "as if she is so interesting that none of us can take our eyes off her! Let me tell you, it is not your looks that got you into our family, it is only your money."

"Yes, the same money that will be used to get you a husband if they can find any man who won't just take the dowry and run off after seeing you and hearing your weird talk."

Always, after one of these exchanges Maria felt ashamed of herself; Rachie was really to be pitied, so anxious to be married, so obsessed by the religion she tried to console herself with, yet somehow she managed always to rile Maria. Rachie alone of all the family, tried to humiliate Maria with oblique references to her antecedents.

Maria had always stood up for herself. Growing up in a multi racial society in Singapore, she often had to contend with both ignorance and prejudice. She had never lacked the ability to give as good as she got. When a girl in the school playground in Singapore had said: "Mary is an English name, you are not English," she had replied: "Mary was the name of the mother of God and she was a Jewish woman who lived long before any Englishwoman even existed! So there!" She was only seven at the time.

Another time, told that she could not be Indian since she was a Christian (Christianity being confused in some Asian minds with British nationality), Maria had proudly retorted that she was a Syrian Christian, a Kerala community of Brahmins who had been Christians since their conversion by St Thomas in the first century, when, as she smugly pointed out, "those who later became the British were running around wild with their skins painted blue." She was little more than ten years old and so could perhaps be forgiven both her arrogance and her unquestioning acceptance of an old myth. Every Syrian Christian liked to believe that his ancestor was one among the group of Namboodiri Brahmins bathing in the river when the Apostle came that way. The story was that

St. Thomas went into the water and threw water up with his hands as the Namboodiris were doing, but the drops he scattered stayed suspended in the air and the men in the river instantly succumbed to the miracle and became Christians.

However, able to take care of herself though she was, Maria could sometimes see the advantage of being where you never had to defend yourself, never needed to explain. It was very tiresome to have continually to say: "No I am not a Tamil and my father is not a coolie;" or, "No, India is not a land of beggars, it may be a poor country now, but it has one of the oldest civilizations." Very tiresome, indeed, so at such times Maria could enter a little into her grandmother's burning desire to 'go home'.

Yet, with her independent nature and free ways, Maria did not fit easily into the Big House household. She was perfectly capable of handling Rachie but for the most part she tried to ignore her because she could not abide her. Although she was closest to her in age, she could not sympathise with Rachie's desperate longing to be married. As for Kuri's elderly uncles and aunts, in her eyes, they bore an uncomfortable resemblance to vultures. It was not their looks, they were ordinary enough, it was the way they gathered at mealtimes, the way in which they seemed to take and to give nothing back. The other Maria, so long ago, had thought the inhabitants of Big House were lordly, magnificent; to young Maria they looked middle-aged and pathetic, without interest, certainly without glamour. They, for their part, were not comfortable with this descendant of a servant whom they all remembered only too well and she looked so much like the Maria Chedathi they could recall. They quickly discovered, however, that there was nothing meek or servile about young Maria's disposition. "Just like that Maria Chedathi," murmured an aunt-in-law, "always thought a lot of herself even when she was only a servant here." They found it difficult to accept that it was Maria who held the purse strings and they were to discover she did not part with money easily. Money is power, as Maria was discovering, and she relished that power.

The fact that Maria had grown up in Malaya, that she had travelled where he had not, both annoyed and fascinated Kuri. He longed to ask her about these places, he who had been nowhere, who was intensely interested in faraway places, countries he had read about and in his mind had invested with flora and fauna of his own imagining. It should have been so simple, the formulating of a question, but to Kuri the asking of a question betokened inferior status, particularly unbefitting the male, the husband. It was his role to explain, to hold forth; it was Maria's to listen, to receive knowledge. Pride stood in his way. He needed to be superior to his wife, it ought to have been he who had experienced the world, not she. It was also wrong that the money belonged to her, was actually in her name. It was unfair! And it made it worse that she was who she was: the descendant of a mere servant in the house. Kuri still resented that fact because he needed to feel that he was worth more. Perhaps he needed a grievance in his life around which to shape all that he could not come to terms with, everything that was lacking. His father's suicide and his mother's inebriation had served that purpose and now he had added Maria.

Kuri had an ambivalent attitude towards women. He had never loved his mother, shying away from her emotional outbursts and her bitterness. Although he did not acknowledge, even to himself, this lack of love, he was filled with a sense of guilt about the relationship and it served to further distance him from Kunjam. Though his grandmother loved him unconditionally and he reciprocated her affection, he knew that it was as his dead father's son that she loved him – when she stumbled over his name, calling him Baben instead of Kuri.

Kuri, too, like Maria, had his dreams, but being male, he was less at ease with them. Uncomfortable with love and a stranger to intimacy, yet he sensed something greater than he was able to encompass, something forever out of his reach.

He was wary of love between man and woman, yet mystified by it; constantly worrying at the mystery of his father's suicide and his mother's vituperation against her husband. What was it that could cause such hatred and such despair in two people? Kuri grew up determined to insulate himself against such emotion. He would never be vulnerable to a woman, he wanted no part of it.

Kuri brought to his marriage this determination, never to allow anyone an emotional upper hand over him; he did not wait to see whether Maria would attempt this or not. What alarmed him was that she had a kind of ruthlessness about her, a hard streak he called it to himself and he quailed before it. When she drew close to his mother he felt as if the two women were in conspiracy against him and it made him uneasy. There was about both women a kind of sexual energy that alarmed him. The other women in Big House were nonentities, all subservient to his grandmother and to their husbands. Women, Kuri felt, should be like that, not able to drive men to suicide or into uncomfortable corners, demanding answers that were not his to give. He had wanted a wife who was beautiful enough to be desirable but who was placid and biddable, making no demands on him except to acknowledge that he was master, who did not seek to enter his mind and control his emotions.

What Kuri really wanted was the easy life. He wanted to be able to recline against the cushions, lie on the veranda overlooking the courtyard where the breeze blew cool, write his poems and be served by a docile woman who did not impinge on him with strident demands and thoughts of her own. He was born too late for that and, as he very well knew, had married the wrong sort of girl. Maria would impinge, she wanted to swallow him up, or so it seemed to him and when his cousin Rachie began to spout sepulchral sayings, they echoed his thoughts uncannily.

To Maria, her husband's behaviour was inexplicable. She could not fathom why he turned away, why sexual intimacy did not lead to mental closeness; why he could enter her body while she could never enter his mind. Each had a different picture of marriage, of their union. And as is usual, it was Maria who gave more thought to it, feared failure, sought more than she felt she had, and put her feelings into words.

Kuri was as unlike Mathen, her father, as a man could be. Maria loved her father and had always loved him in an unquestioning easy way. He was the perfect example of a self made man, full of practical ability, never afraid of hard work and because of his phenomenal success, completely at ease with himself. Kuri, who might be said to have it all, brains, breeding, prestige, was by comparison an angular personality full of complexes and sharp edges.

Maria, despite being brought up outside India, had been well tutored in Indian ways. Her grandmother had seen to that. There had always been a clear-cut line between what her friends might do and what was permitted to her. "Why?" Maria had often stormed and "That is the way," her grandmother would reply, implacable. She had resented this and had, of course, circumvented grandmother and tradition as often as she could but not without feelings of guilt that had made her sulky and what the elder Maria had termed 'unbiddable'.

"It's a wonder I'm not schizophrenic," the young Maria would shout then and now, married, she tried to explain this feeling to Kuri, tried to explain why in some ways she was not, and could not be, a traditional wife. She did not think he understood, she was not sure he did not wilfully misunderstand. Strangely, it was his mother, Kunjam, who sympathized.

"Men understand no problems but their own," she said. "They expect so much from women, but they treat us as of little account. If we step out of line they stone us and if we do not trouble them they place us where they cannot see us clearly and they call it worship, but they never try to know our pain and help us to deal with it. Who in this house has looked into my face, let alone into my heart? My husband killed himself once but they kill me every day. They said he was unhappy, but unhappiness was not for him alone. Any way he could not deal with it, hanged himself like a common criminal. Tchah! What good was he? A coward who feared life and himself; yet his picture hangs like that of a god and the family worships before it. And me? I live with my pain and I am an outcast! Untouchable."

Big House, Maria was discovering, was not a happy house.

15

Despite the money set apart from Maria's dowry, marriage was not immediately forthcoming for Kuri's cousin Rachie who continued to exhibit the stigmata on her palms and feet, which bled on high days and holidays and particularly when she was crossed in anything; she also continued to see visions in unlikely places. Usually these apparitions were Jesus and Mary his mother, who accosted her all over the house at unpropitious moments and in odd places. However, the last such vision had been a departure from the ordinary: it had occurred in the new bathroom that Maria had installed and Jesus and Mary had arrived accompanied by an unnamed third party who seemed to be trying to tell Rachie something; she thought it had to do with the new bride. Something, Rachie thought, that was not good, not good at all and she had looked malevolently at Maria.

Maria, in a bad mood after an argument with Kuri, shouted at her: "You are hysterical. You should see a doctor and then find yourself a husband." The marks of stigmata almost immediately began to bleed and Rachie's mother accused Maria of blasphemy.

Sternly, the grandmother spoke: "We will not have this kind of disruption in our house. Rachie will see a doctor, but you Maria will apologise to her and the rest of you," turning to her assembled sons and daughters-in-law, "will all hold your tongues."

Later the old lady called Maria to her room where the untouchable woman always known by her community name, Chauathi, never given a personal name, was engaged in massaging the mistress's legs with hot oil. The old lady motioned Maria to sit beside her on the bed but she hung back, sulky, anticipating a scolding.

"I am not angry," she said reassuringly, "you only spoke the truth as you saw it. Poor Rachie should be married and with the money you have brought it should have been possible, but word has got out about the marks on her hands and feet, about her visions and people are saying she is mad. What can one do? Sometimes I am so weary..." she broke off and her normally stern face looked so unhappy that impulsively, Maria seized the oil from Chauathi who was glad to stand back and let her take over. And from that day it became customary for Maria to massage Kuri's grandmother's legs. Even though there had been little overt warmth between them, it seemed to please the old lady and Chauathi was wont to say: "The young Mistress has a healing touch," as she poured hot oil into Maria's palm. At first, the hot oil poured into her palm had reminded Maria of the hot sugar balls her grandmother had had to make for this family and she had been cold and distant with the old woman. After some time, however, it became apparent to Maria that the old lady wanted to talk to her, to lessen some of the distance between them. Still later, she realized, it was the old woman's purpose to make her aware of the responsibility that was being gradually but inexorably passed on to her.

"There is always someone in this world to shoulder responsibility when it is needed. I was one of those; only a few years older than you are now, I was the Mistress of the Big House and soon, a middle-aged woman. There was no one but me and I was never able to let the burden drop."

Another time she said: "You think Kunjam is to be pitied, don't you? Perhaps so. But people become what they are. The weak remain weak unless they fight to change themselves. Everyone has to change somewhat, life demands that of most if not all of us. Do you think I was always the same? When I was young I too dreamed of all those things young girls dream about.... Many things in life change a person but none more than marriage. This is especially true of women, although men change too in different ways. I changed. I hardened. This house, Big House, would not have been what it was if it were not for me and the women who came before me. It is we who have given our lives to it. Look what happened when for a few short years I had to let go."

The old lady sighed. She looked at her faithful maid kneeling by the bed. "Chauathi here has seen so much change in her lifetime. There was a time when she could not let her shadow fall in front of a high caste person, when she had to speak only with her mouth covered. She hasn't lost that habit even now, although the times are changing. If only she were able to tell it all, to explain how the world has changed. How old are you now, girl?"Maria, startled, realized that the question was addressed to the old servant and not to her.

Chauathi smiled. "Who can say, Mistress? Who bothers with such things for such as I? I do not even know which day I was born on; it is of no importance. I am old and when you go, I will go too."

"Our experiences, however wonderful or terrible they may be, are nothing in the telling. Even poor uneducated Chauathi knows that. Kuri thinks that the language in which we clothe our ideas is important and it is true, the clever word can capture a fleeting interest, but the colour, the agony, the frustration, will have gone. Nobody is really interested in another's experiences. That is why no one learns from what went before. Kuri is a good boy but he has had much to contend with from an early age. Perhaps we spoilt him a little to make up to him for the loss of his father." An expression of pain crossed her face.

"We women are not as strong as men but we have stamina, the ability to carry on, to endure. Seek within yourself for strength and I believe you will find it. Your grandmother had that quality of endurance and it stood her in good stead. I pray that you have it too for as I come to the end of my days I realize that in this life that is all that matters. It is what will see you through. Go child," she said, "go to sleep and may God bless you."

As Maria turned to go she heard the old woman murmur: "It is all such a pity, such a waste, but maybe Chauathi, this time, God willing, it will come right."

To which the maid replied: "Everything goes forward, *Thampuraati*, whether we wish it or not. The old have to stand back and watch the young take over and they must do things in their own way. We cannot stop it. The young Mistress is a good girl and she is strong like that grandmother of hers. She will look after Big House." Both the women sighed and the door closed behind Maria.

16

Our mothers," said Kunjam, "want for us not what we might want, but what they wanted for themselves. Unfortunately, we are all different and our different lives make us ever more different." Maria could not help wondering whether her mother-in-law had not imbibed rather too freely from her medicine bottle. There was a pause and then Kunjam said: "Ask someone to describe a tree and they will answer green. But a tree is not all green or rather not always the same green. There are touches of yellow, of dark and light green and, of course, brown. People are like that, different and changing. The girl who came into this house so many years ago is not the same as the woman I am now, living in this house. You too will change as I did. That is the only real freedom we have, to change with time, unnoticed." She spoke abstractedly, breaking off, and then speaking again. "You know, I always thought that looks were important; I could not imagine being a woman who looked in the mirror only to see if her hair was combed flat. Looks are important for a woman. Yet isn't it strange that a good looking woman needs a mirror or the eyes of other people to reveal her beauty to her?" She paused and was silent for so long, staring at a tree, that Maria wondered (as she often did) whether her mother-in-law had not gone off into an alcohol-induced doze. But then she spoke again, in a dreaming voice: "My grandmother, I still remember her so well, was a beautiful woman. My grandfather was an ogre. He fought with everyone, even his only son, allowed no one their own way. They used to say my grandmother was like a beautiful bird without a song. They also said her husband loved her dearly because she 'was a good wife' and when she died he went into paroxysms of grief. He would not let her be buried in church, he wanted her to be buried in the house where he could keep her always with him. It never occurred to him that she might want, at least in death, to get away from him! It was the only fight he lost. But now, sitting here, I wonder who was that woman really, that good wife, good woman? It seems to me that a woman who does not stand up to her husband, who never lets pain, anger or grief out of the house, is what everyone calls 'a good woman'. A woman who is difficult, who will not accept what everyone tells her, is 'mad'. 'These trouble making women,' they say, women say, 'only make trouble for all of us.' The quiet, the good woman, whom no one notices particularly, is most frightened because she has much to lose. If you think about it," she went on, "we women are like mirrors in which men see themselves reflected at twice their natural size and we believe what we see."

Maria liked to hear Kunjam talk and now as she listened to her she realized that there is in women, there was in her, a vein of anger. She saw how the strands of families wove themselves this way and that, the warp and the weft, the dark and the light, lying across from each other and always the lighter strands were the women. "You know," said Maria, "there is a Malay saying 'don't think there are no crocodiles in calm waters'. It is a saying that suits this family, on the outside so traditional, so ordinary, so sort of seething somehow underneath it all."

Kunjam laughed and the laugh was not pleasant. "You don't know even the half of it, my child," she said, "that's why they are so afraid to let me out of their sight, fearful of what I might say, not sure whether I will let the cat out of the bag. Some day I will, when I am ready. I shall make the old woman suffer as she has made me suffer."

Maria stared at her fascinated. "What do you mean?" she asked curiously.

"All in good time," Kunjam replied and chuckled, "I shall give everyone something to think about before I go."

"Go? Go where?" Maria was bewildered.

"Depart this earth where my only happiness was as a little girl." Kunjam paused and frowned, twisting a strand of hair and suddenly, fleetingly, Maria caught a glimpse of her as she must have looked as a child.

"It is not a good thing to have been a happy child," said Kunjam, "one should not want only to go back when the law of life is to go forward and anyway, as a girl, one's whole purpose was to look forward to one's marriage, and see where that landed me."

Maria hesitated, then she said: "You should not keep thinking of the past..." In her own ears her words reminded her of her grandmother and she knew that she sounded sententious.

Kunjam cut in, quick as a whiplash: "What then should I be thinking of, the happy present? Of being ignored by my only child, living like a stranger in a house where everyone hates me but will not let me go? Or should I be thinking of the future when I will lie in that graveyard of the church where both of us got married, lie beside my husband who never in life wanted to lie with me?" She rose, stumbling and clumsy, to her feet clutching her medicine bottle, now empty.

From the shadows of the inner rooms her maid emerged like another shadow to escort her mistress inside. She brought with her Kunjam's breakfast, long rows of *puttoo*, steamed rice flour bordered by pearly white grated coconut, eaten with small finger length bananas. There was a ghostly chuckle as Kunjam paused in the dark corridor, hanging back from her maid's arm, and Maria heard her say: "That child thinks she can teach her grandmother to suck eggs! The idea of telling me not to think of the past..." Kunjam came back into the room and once more resumed her seat beside Maria. "You are right, Maria," she said, sitting down and beginning to eat, mashing the bananas into the steamed *puttoo* which the maid set out in front of her, "I have lived in the past and can do nothing else, but you must not do that. My marriage is irrelevant now, do you know, I can scarcely recall Baben's, my husband's face, yet I cannot let go. But if you have any sense, learn to let go, live as you just told me to, in the present and the future. Keep moving onwards, although this house and its occupants may make that difficult."

"I don't think that's right either," responded Maria, "one needs to know why something happens, to work out why and what one should have done."

"Believe me, if you can do it, the best thing is to put it all behind you and move on, that way you may not suffer as I have done." She paused for a moment and then said: "Some people are like this *puttoo*, they do not land on the plate long, straight, unbroken, the rice flour joined at the seams by neat layers of coconut. No, instead they break as they are pushed out of the mould and crumble into an unsightly mess."

"But," Maria rejoined, "it tastes the same, doesn't it?"

"Perhaps," Kunjam said, "but broken *puttoo* is not a success."

Was it Baben she referred to or herself?

That night Maria said to Kuri. "Why do you ignore your mother? You should talk to her sometimes, show her that you love her."

"Of course I love her," snapped Kuri, "is she not my mother? But it is not easy to talk to her, she is so emotional."

"That is because she drinks and she drinks because she is unhappy and has nothing else."

"She takes medicine. What do you mean by saying she drinks? Of course, there is some alcohol in the *kashayam,* the ayurvedic medicine she takes, but that does not mean she drinks." Kuri's tone was angry, but he avoided Maria's eyes.

Maria crossed over to stand in front of him, forcing him to look at her. "She drinks and it is alcohol in that medicine bottle. That bottle has not held medicine for many a long year I'd be prepared to bet. Everyone in this house knows it but pretend they do not! Don't you try and fool me."

"Well and if so, what can I do about it?" muttered Kuri.

"Instead of writing so much about love and pain and suffering in those books of yours, try and find out what goes on in your mother's mind. That is real and important."

"What do you know?" sneered Kuri. "I don't expect you to understand what I write or think about. How could you?"

"What do you mean 'how could I'? What are you trying to say?" Maria's antenna, always sensitive to slights and aspersions on her antecedents, was angled to pick up an insult.

"Nothing," answered Kuri gruffly, turning away, "I don't want to discuss it, that's all." "I suppose you mean I'm not clever enough for you, only my money is good enough," sneered Maria, hating herself for stooping so low, yet determined to wound.

"I wondered how soon it would be before you brought that

up," said Kuri. "Well let me tell you, your money may have bought this house and our name but it has not bought me. You will never own me, try as you might."

"Oh Kuri, I don't want to own you. I just want to love and be loved. I came in here to tell you to be kinder to your mother. She's a very unhappy woman and I feel sorry for her. I just thought you might be kinder to her, talk to her sometimes. That's all." Maria, reared in a loving home where she had never known any real strife or hatred, did not know how to cope in this house so full of undercurrents of hate, hostility, pent up sexual frustration.

She had intended to tell Kuri that she was pregnant, that she hoped the coming child would make them happy, draw them together. She said nothing because some vague superstitious fear made her think that good news must not be told at a bad moment. So she lay on her bed with her back to Kuri and said not a word. Kuri, for his part, lay pretending to be asleep because he did not know how to deal with the two warring sides of himself. Part of him would have liked to embrace Maria, to open himself to experience that he knew lay above and beyond himself, which he wanted to seize and could not. What seemed to come more naturally to him was rejection, both of his mother and his wife, both of whom wanted from him what he could not give, did not have. Both women seemed unable to release him from his prison and he resented them for it. He had never in all his life faced himself and found that self wanting. However, he probably sensed that there was something more and that he did not possess it.

Whatever Maria had been told, no one had ever told her that marriage could be this pathetic, ludicrous business where two people who should have been closer than anything in this world, could lie as far from each other all night as the marriage bed would allow. How was it possible, she was often to ask herself as the years passed, for two people to live together for so long and know so little about each other? Or so much, yet not the really vital things?

17

Maria's pregnancy was uneventful, even enjoyable, because everyone made a fuss of her. Perhaps because he was pleased, Kuri relaxed and drew closer to his wife; they talked of the baby to come and allowed themselves to dream a little.

"Things will be different for him," said Kuri, "he will not have the hard time I had growing up."

"It may be a girl," said Maria, "and if it is, I shall never force her to do what I want; she will be free."

"I think," said Kunjam, "you are already deciding things for the baby, we all do that. Everyone wants what they think is best for their children. But when I was expecting Kuri, my husband was already dead and he was cursed with a widowed mother. I never enjoyed motherhood," she smiled, "let's hope I will enjoy being a grandmother."

As Maria's stomach began to swell (and everyone said she was bigger than most) she was aware of hostile emanations and correctly assumed that they came from Rachie and her mother. The latter bemoaned the fate of her daughter, unmarried and seemingly destined to go to her grave a spinster. Rachie herself said little, but Maria was uneasily aware of the girl's eyes always upon her and of the malice in their depths.

"I'm just glad I'm as strong as an ox", said Maria, "if I were feeling ill, being sick and uncomfortable, I could not have endured it. Besides which, with all her talk of ghosts and spirits I might well have begun to think she was putting a jinx on me." She was glad to be able to depart to her father and grandmother in Pallisseri to await the childbirth.

Maria bore twins, a boy and a girl. The boy, everyone said, looked like his mother, while the little girl took after Kuri and his family and perhaps because of that, he gave her his heart. His mother was delighted with her grandchildren; although Kuri turned away, pretending not to hear, it had disturbed him greatly when Kunjam said, almost as if she were speaking to herself: "The shining eyes of one's child can show what one's mother's eyes might have been like had she ever been happy." The birth of children meant that Maria and Kuri were now considered to have reached a settled stage in their married lives. They were no longer just a young couple; theirs was now deemed to be a family.

The birth of Maria's twins, however, brought about other disturbance, not entirely unforeseen. No sooner did Maria return with her babies to Veloorkada from her father's house in Pallisseri where she had gone for her confinement as custom dictated than Rachie graduated from divine visions to seeing ghosts. At first she claimed only to see unidentified young men wandering around the house and nobody paid any particular attention although, perhaps, in the light of later events they rather wished they had. Her grandmother had redoubled her efforts to find a suitable bridegroom for the girl, but she had not been successful. Rachie was not particularly good looking and gossip about her visions, her stigmata, (despite all attempts by the family to stifle it), coupled with whispers about Kunjam and Baben effectively drove away most suitors.

One day, soon after Maria returned with her babies, when the whole family was absorbed in them, cooing and clucking and tracing resemblances, Rachie began to claim that the young man whose ghost kept appearing to her was none other than her uncle Baben. He had manifested himself before, but had not deigned to speak and so she had, she said, not been sure of his identity. This time, however, he had unburdened himself to Rachie. There was nothing wonderful about the fact that she could describe a man who had died before she was born. Besides the large portrait of him in the main room, there were quite a few photographs as well. What was disturbing was that she claimed that Baben had told her that he wanted the truth known about his death and that he was unhappy about his son's marriage. Rachie declared that Baben had said that Maria was too much like Kunjam; she claimed that he had said: "She will eat Kuri alive just as I was eaten alive."

Rachie chose a moment when the whole family was gathered together to impart this particular message from beyond and she watched eagerly, like a vulture hovering over its prey, as they digested it along with their meal. To Maria, they all, all the uncles and aunts, looked like scavenging birds bent over Rachie's juicy gobbet of news served up with their meal. Consternation broke out among uncles, aunts and cousins. Everyone looked first, furtively, at Kunjam and then at Maria and finally in open fear at the old lady.

She was the first to speak; pushing back her chair, she said before either Kunjam or Maria could say anything: "Rachie, you will go to your room and stay there. I shall send for the priest. The rest of you, do not speak of this to anyone and do not discuss it even among yourselves." She signalled to her daughter who began to wheel her away from the table. Rachie burst into tears and began to rock hysterically to and fro, all the time peering through her fingers at her distraught relatives. Her mother ran to her, but froze at a look from her mother-in-law. Kunjam and Maria had both risen from the table, but it was the former who spoke first: "Those who cannot live are 'eaten alive' and then must return to speak to those who like themselves are half creatures, not daring what they most want to do," she spoke calmly enough, but then she looked at her mother-in-law and her voice sharpened as she added: "One of these days I see that the truth about your beloved son will have to be told. Not by some spectral creature that lives in the sick fancies of a neurotic girl, but by me. Yes, both you and I know the truth about Baben. I finally discovered it when I ceased to be the ignorant young girl who came here to be his wife," then she turned and walked away and there was an unaccustomed dignity about her.

Maria remained standing and she turned on Kuri who sat looking at no one. "How can you sit there and let this half witted cousin of yours insult me, hiding behind ghosts and visions? And who am I to eat you alive when you can do the job yourself?" she asked furiously.

Kuri said nothing, aimlessly rolling a ball of rice between his fingers, but his grandmother spoke: "That is enough Maria. You will not trade insults in my presence. Rachie is sick and we must treat her for her sickness...."

She was interrupted by a ghostly chuckle from the shadows beyond the door; Kunjam stood there, ever the eavesdropper. "Well," she said, "when I was young they did not call it sickness. Rachie wants what every young woman wants and she cannot have it. First she had no dowry to get her a husband and now that the money is there, no man can be found to take a girl who is half mad. She is not the first to suffer in this way and if we all go on as we do with our dowries and our arranged marriages, she will not be the last," saying which, Kunjam turned and walked away. The priest was sent for; he arrived with his *kapiyar*, the sexton, swinging censers filled with incense, ringing a bell, intoning prayers of exorcism, exhorting the devil to depart from Rachie. The gathered family intoned the responses in funereal tones, beseeching the devil to leave Rachie alone. Throughout the ceremony Rachie's mother wept copiously but the girl herself sat with a fixed smile on her face, "Delighted," said Maria to Kunjam, "to be the centre of attention."

"It is what she needs. She should have gone out and taken a job as her other two cousins did. Surely it is better to earn your living than to live as she does, hoping and waiting?"

"I liked the bit about the Gadarene swine, but let's hope Rachie's devils haven't gone into any of the poor animals!"

Kunjam laughed with Maria, then she sighed: "Like most of us, the poor girl does not know how to seize happiness unless it is arranged for and placed in her lap," she said.

She was wrong. One morning Rachie was not to be found and her mother ran weeping to the old lady. "You see, now you see what has happened to my poor little girl? She is not to be found, I am sure she is dead," she beat her breast and wailed: "Come back Rachie, don't go away and leave us like this." Her weeping and wailing resounded through the old house and it seemed to Maria to echo from the walls in terrible ululation.

The old lady gave orders that the well and the fishponds be dragged, but to no avail. There was no sign of Rachie's body. "If she went into the river where it runs fast and deep, her body will not be found for days, perhaps never," the family whispered among themselves.

The days passed and everyone was sure that Rachie was dead. "Another suicide?" the family whispered among themselves, "what is happening? What is this curse placed on us?"Maria felt guilty, remembering the way she had screamed at the girl, accused her of being mad. "I wonder how she did it," she said to Kuri. "I wonder if her body will ever turn up."

Kuri had written a poem about his cousin, full of symbolism and dark imagery and one of the leading magazines had accepted it. He was very happy and so he smiled and said: "It is better this way. Perhaps she is at peace now, poor girl."

It was a great shock when suddenly Rachie reappeared. "She drove up in a taxi," Kunjam's maid told Maria and Kunjam. "She got out as calm and cool as you like. There was someone in the taxi with her but I could not see who it was. Looked like a man," she added portentously.

Rachie was closeted with her grandmother while the family, excluded, hung about outside straining to hear what went on inside the room. Rachie's father was finally summoned and went into his mother's room, leaving his wife sobbing and beating her breast outside. Later the old lady appeared in the doorway from where she glared at her assembled family. Rachie stood behind her, a foolish smile on her face, while her eyes sought those of the family who stood there, perhaps seeking their support.

Her grandmother was clearly in the grip of great emotion

but as usual, she kept a tight rein on herself. "Rachie, as you can all see, is not dead." Almost to herself, she added: "Perhaps it would have been better.... but henceforth she is dead to me and she will never set foot in this house again while I am alive to see it."

Rachie pushed herself forward, almost elbowing her grandmother aside; she smiled defiantly at her relatives and struck an attitude, one hand protectively placed over her belly. The old lady went back into her room and shut the door with a loud bang.

"Oh!" exclaimed Rachie, "I do not care what anyone thinks and no one can make me do anything I do not want to."

It was left to Rachie's father to break the news that his daughter had been having an affair with one of the workmen whom Maria had brought in to refurbish the house, that she had eloped with him and that she was pregnant. The man had sent Rachie to demand her dowry without which he refused to legalise the situation. In fact, he was waiting outside in the taxi. Every word that was dragged reluctantly from Rachie's father was punctuated by his wife's wailing.

"In the old days," said Chacko, "we would have horse whipped him. Today he and his like have us in their power." His brother replied: "In the old days Rachie would have been married long ago and this would never have happened."

Rachie could not be left unwed, not with a child on the way. The honour of the Big House was in serious jeopardy.

The marriage was performed, the dowry given and Rachie left the Big House never to return until after her grandmother's death.

The Big House reeled from the blow and the indomitable old lady, the Mistress, called Maria to her: "Child," she said, "what is to become of us all? What have we done wrong that we have come to this? Bring up your children carefully, Maria and pray God to lift this curse from our family."

"I don't think there is any curse," Maria replied. "Rachie was brought up to think there was no one good enough for a girl from Big House and then she found this was not so. The only important thing is money. It is a pity that when there was enough to pay her dowry, she could not marry because people had begun to talk badly about the family. It is our society that is at fault and, of course, Rachie is also a very silly girl. Had she waited and not talked so much nonsense, I am sure you would have found someone suitable for her."

"It is not so simple," the old woman responded, "but then, life seems simple when one is young. Everything seems so clear cut. When you are as old as I, you will find that everything grows hazier. But one thing does not change and that is honour. The Big House is passing to you, child, to Kuri and you; guard it, look after it. There is nothing more important than family name and honour. I entrust these to you, I can do no more."

Maria said nothing, but she wondered if other things, as important as family honour, had not been neglected for too long.

'More love and kindness is what Big House needs and they need to know that they are no longer the important people they once were.' She said nothing, however, for she knew the old grandmother would never agree. It was too late to try and make her see where everything had gone wrong; but it was not too late for the rest of them. There would have to be a day of reckoning.

18

The family of the Big House never really recovered from the blow of Rachie's elopement with a workman and her subsequent marriage, although the marriage was, in its way, a happy one blessed in the shortest possible time with a number of offspring. That the first of these chose to make its appearance less than five months after the wedding caused the Big House greater humiliation.

The grandmother became noticeably feebler and as her physical strength appeared to wane so the bitterness of her tongue seemed to increase. One day loud voices were heard from her room and to the surprise of the listeners it was Kunjam's voice that could be heard, Kunjam who had never been in her mother-in-law's room since Baben died, telling her mother-in-law: "Lies have been told for too long and secrets kept. It has been easy to blame me and keep your son's name sweet. But I have had enough now. Surely, I said to myself, if that poor creature Rachie is capable of so much boldness, why should I alone be weak and fearful. I will tell the truth now and you cannot stop me any more."

"I will stop you," the old woman answered, "if it is the last thing I do and if you push me, it probably will be the last thing I do. But at my age I am not afraid of death. Indeed, I would welcome it now, but I will not let you destroy this family again. In young Maria's hands this house will prosper again, is already beginning to prosper and I will never let you sink our name in shame. Do not think that I am too old to stop you; this house and all it stands for is Kuri's and Maria's inheritance and their children's after them. You are nobody and have been nobody for a very long time."

"Don't underestimate me, I warn you. I have suffered at your hands for long enough, but I am finished with all that and remember, I have nothing to lose."

"Do you care nothing for your own son?" There was a change in the older woman's voice that suggested conciliation. Perhaps, after all, she did not underestimate Kunjam, knew that she was a dangerous adversary as, indeed, people are who no longer care.

"I now care for nobody," Kunjam replied, "but if my son is half a man he will survive what I have to say and go on with his life. If not, it doesn't matter any way. You saw to it that I lost my son a long time ago. I hope the son I gave birth to is not the poor weakling your son was and I will grant you this, he is luckier in his wife than yours was with his, even though her family consists of nobodies." She paused and in the silence the family pressed closer to the door the better to overhear what went on inside the room.

"I was ill equipped to deal with what I found. I was little more than a child when I came here to Big House and children are supposed to be innocent. But I was not only innocent, I was ignorant."

"I warn you Kunjam," the ferocity was back in the older woman's voice, "I will fight to stop you even if it kills me..."

"Or me?" Kunjam's voice was teasing; the listeners gathered outside the door somehow knew that they were intended to hear, that at least one of the two women knew that there was an audience beyond the entrance.

Later, when disaster befell, they were to ask themselves why Kunjam had spoken so loudly, why she had stood so close to the door, why she had wanted the whole house to overhear what she said.

To Maria, Kunjam said: "If anything happens to me, be sure you do not let them hush it up. Make sure that it is investigated."

"What do you mean?" Maria was abstracted; the twins were teething and she had been up most of the night with them. "What is going to happen to you? You should not speak in riddles if you want my help. You have not been drinking, have you?" There was honesty, at least about that, between the two women. The container, the mud brown bottle, might still be called a medicine bottle, but for a very long time there had been no ambiguity about its contents. Long before Maria had come to Big House, it had ceased to be medicine.

"No, I have not been drinking. For what is about to happen I have to keep a clear head. It is not easy for me; I suffer when I don't have my 'medicine', but this is too important for me to bungle..."

"I told you," Maria was irritable, "if there is something you want me to know or do, you have to tell me clearly."

"There is nothing I want you to do except this: if anything should happen to me, make sure there is a full investigation. Don't let them, her, the old woman, get away with hushing things up as she did before. No," as Maria opened her mouth to say something, "I am not going to say another word. Just remember what I have told you. Maybe I am too dangerous now to be allowed to live." She turned and went into her room and shut the door. Maria heard her pulling the heavy bar into place that locked the door and this was unusual in the daytime. Was Kunjam going mad? She had always been unbalanced, Maria had recognised that from the beginning...The twins wailed and Maria, attending to them, forgot her mother-in-law's words. She was to remember them in full later on but by then there was nothing to be done.

Kunjam continued to behave very strangely. She started calling in a cat at mealtimes to which she first fed a morsel of everything with which she was served. The cat, once a thin and starveling creature, soon grew fat and glossy. The family watched this daily performance and said nothing. Only Maria remarked that it might be more fair were Kunjam to divide her food among all the yard animals; she was the champion of all the half starved creatures that hung about the yard and outhouses.

"I am not running an animal charity," Kunjam replied. "I'm just making sure that everything I put into my mouth is good for my health."

Maria looked at Kuri to see whether he had marked his mother's strange words and behaviour, but Kuri avoided her eyes. He would not ask his mother, as he knew Maria wanted him to, what she meant. He did not want to know and he was skilled in avoiding what he knew would unravel in front of him in a mess of loose ends that he did not wish to tie up. He knew that this refusal of his to confront anything that was likely to be unpleasant or difficult infuriated his wife, but that had become his way and he adhered to it. Peace at all costs was his maxim.

The family, silent but watchful, gained the impression that Kunjam thought her food might be tampered with, but no one reasoned with her, no one laughed at the apparent absurdity; they, too, skilled in avoiding trouble, looked away and were silent, only remembering when it was too late.

Big House now was an even more desperate place. Rachie's mother mourned her daughter's absence audibly and would not be comforted. She constantly begged her husband to try and make his mother rescind her decision to deny Rachie admission to the house. When Rachie's first baby arrived, as the poor woman put it, her eyes sliding away, 'prematurely', her pleas that Rachie be forgiven were redoubled. Her husband, grey and worn, skilled in his own way at avoiding trouble, went more often to the teashop where a bottle of rum kept specially for him comforted his sore heart.

Kuri and Maria, meanwhile, were discovering that parenthood has a way of uniting two people despite themselves. Two people cannot battle through teething and sleepless nights, colic, chicken pox, measles and mumps, without barriers coming down. Shared pride over the tottering first steps, the first words, is a joyous and special thing for two people to enjoy. A child is an amalgam of both parents and in loving one's child one loves in him one's partner as well as oneself. All love is in some form a kind of egoism, Maria thought, as she held her babies and admired their perfection.

'Perhaps,' said Maria to herself, 'devotion and caring are the real important things?' Wistfulness was betokened by the questioning note. Maybe, she thought, not everyone falls in love.

She had, however, asserted herself and brought back from her father's house her dog Bimbo. The large alsatian immediately threw the Big House family into pandemonium, striking terror into the hearts of elderly uncles and aunts. Kuri tried to insist that Bimbo should go back to Pallisseri because it was a danger to the twins, but Maria was adamant. "That dog is important to me. He makes me happy. Do you not want me to be happy? If there was something that made you happy, I would not prevent you from having it." There was no possible reply to that.

Bimbo, being an expert on human psychology as so many animals are (and need to be in a world not arranged for them), not only made himself indispensable to the twins, but set about wooing Kuri and before a year was out, was more Kuri's dog than Maria's and this had its own effect on their relationship. Maria was very glad that she had stood up for her rights instead of acting like a martyr. In many ways, almost unconsciously, she was influenced by Kunjam, whose words reinforced her own natural tendency towards independence and equality. "Seize what you truly want," said Kunjam, "for if you do not take, no one will give. If you lie down looking like a hank of coir, they make you into a doormat and wipe their feet all over you!"

Kunjam every now and then continued to throw out veiled hints about her death and the possibility that she would be silenced because at last she meant to tell the world the truth. The family, by and large, discounted her words, most of them believing that drink had finally destroyed her brain. It was, as Kunjam had said, so much easier to say that a woman was mad, uncontrollable; there was little to be done about madness. Only the little granddaughter, Elishuba, loved her grandmother unconditionally; "mad," she lisped, mimicking, "good mad," and her grandmother embraced her, the smell of toddy already familiar to the little girl, strong on her breath.

19

They found Kunjam lying dead at the bottom of the attic ladder, a pathetic broken heap. Tightly clenched in one hand was a piece of canvas, old and rotten. It looked like a part of a painting. It was Chacko who found her; elderly, with a weak heart and fastidious personality, it looked for a few moments as if his own death from shock would follow shortly. Kunjam's maid, however, was quickly on the scene, throwing herself down by the prostrate body of her mistress and wailing so loudly as to bring the entire family running to stand aghast around the body.

Looking surreptitiously about her, making sure that the family had gathered around, she began to scream: "She has been killed, my poor mistress. She knew it was going to happen, she warned me, but I was unable to save her. She told me she was going to tell everything, the truth, she said the Old Mistress would try and stop her." She wrung her hands and wept but had anyone cared to notice it might have been observed that she spoke mainly to Maria.

"Shut your mouth. Let us have no more of your screaming," the old lady had been wheeled in by her daughter. "You forget yourself," she said to the maid, "I want you to pack your things and be out of here before the day ends."

The maid, however, stood her ground. "I will not go until my mistress has been buried. I will stay with her until then and I will see justice done. I came with her when she was married and I will not leave her alone now." She looked the old lady in the eye and the family stood silent, horrified and amazed by her temerity. Not one of them had ever stood up to the old lady and they could not believe the servant's courage. "You cannot make me leave," the maid added, "these are no longer the old days when you people could do as you please. The times have changed and we poor people have rights too. We also know what we can do and I can tell you, you would not like it. It is the people's government now and I know where to go to get my rights. If you want me to go and I will only go when I am ready, you will have to pay me to go."

The two women faced each other over the body of Kunjam and it was the aristocratic old lady who looked away first. "Kuri," she said to her grandson, "see to your mother."

Kuri bent over his mother's body, gingerly feeling for her pulse in her outstretched arm. "How could it have happened?" he asked, speaking almost to himself, "what was she doing up in the *thattumbaram*?" There was nothing in the attic except old things stored away.

There was no reply from the assembled family, although one or two of them moved closer to the body and indicated the object clutched in Kunjam's hand.

Maria knelt beside the body and gently turned it over. Kunjam's eyes were open and staring, her face contused, but there was the faintest smile discernible. Gently, almost without thinking, Maria's fingers moved over her mother-in-law's face and closed her eyes. She looked more closely at the roll of canvas in Kunjam's hand; it was dusty and covered with cobwebs and had clearly come from the attic. One end was jagged and torn.

"We should go up to the attic and see," Maria suggested and began to climb the steep uneven ladder. She felt dazed, moving like an automaton. She could not believe that Kunjam was lying down there, dead. Her husband followed her and behind him came the uncles and aunts, leaving behind the old lady and her son Chacko who was bent over the railings, gasping for breath.

The body lay where it was.

Kunjam's maid scampered up the stairs, overtaking Maria, almost pushing her aside. "See," she said, pointing to the trapdoor, which lay open and gaining entrance into the gloom of the long attic with low ceiling, "my mistress was looking for something when she was disturbed and pushed down the steps." Several old boxes had been moved and one trunk stood open, its contents tossed around. A piece of what looked like the same canvas the dead woman held in her hand, lay on the floor by the ladder, as if torn off.

"That thing in her hand," Maria said, picking up the fallen piece, "perhaps we should look at it." She glanced at Kuri as she spoke. He had gone very pale at the maid's ominous words.

"These are Baben's things," said Verghese, "they were placed here when he... after my brother died. His paintings and letters and other such things. Some of his paintings were torn then. I remember thinking he must have torn them up before he killed...er...died. Mother preserved everything as it was. Nobody has looked at any of it in all these years. Mother had them placed here. Why would Kunjam want them after all these years? Most of it must have rotted away by now."

There was no answer from any of the family but the maid pushed forward: "Because there was proof here of what she wanted known after all these years. She said that at last the truth must be known. My mistress was blamed long enough for what was not her fault." She swung round to Maria: "She told you so, I heard her, she told you to see that if anything happened to her you must have it investigated. It is your duty."

The family turned to look at Maria who had been studying the piece of canvas she had picked up, peering at it in the gloom of the attic, lit only by a single skylight. The uncles and aunts reminded her of a herd of goats as they stood there staring at her, their heads swinging to and fro, and suddenly she found it all unbearably funny and began to laugh, doubling up, gasping for breath. Then her laughter turned to tears; sinking to her knees in front of the open trunk she wept for Kunjam, her mother-in-law, who had been her only real friend in the Big House.

Kuri knelt beside her and tentatively, uncertainly, he put an arm around her. Without a moment's hesitation, Maria turned and went into his arms. For a second, Kuri did not move and then his other arm went round her and tightened in an embrace and he too wept for his mother. It was a moment that neither of them would ever forget.

One of the aunts pulled out something that lay a little behind the trunk and in the dim half-light she examined it. "What is it you have there?" Verghese, her husband, asked.

"It looks like drawings of young..." she hesitated and peered more closely at it, settling her glasses more firmly on her nose. "It looks like young women but really, I think they are drawings of...," she broke off uncertainly and looked at her husband in puzzlement. The others crowded round her to look.

Maria raised her head from her husband's shoulder and she whispered: "Your mother was always hinting at something... she seemed to suggest that your father..." she broke off, unsure of how to tell him. The maid was beside them: "Your father," she told Kuri, "liked men not women. It was his secret. He tried to hide it from everyone and he married your mother but it did not work. Your mother thought at first he loved some other woman. At one time she even fancied it might be your grandmother, she was good looking enough," she said to Maria, "but finally she guessed the truth. He killed himself because of it and you, all of you," she wheeled round to include the family who almost cowered behind the open trunks, "blamed her. At last she wanted the truth known and she was killed to stop her."

"You don't know what you are saying!" Kuri exclaimed.

"Then look at this," the maid shouted and snatching away the drawings from the aunt and uncle, she brandished them in front of Kuri. Maria, looking over his shoulder, saw grotesque drawings of women, of harpy like female figures snatching at male genitalia. She heard Kuri draw in his breath and: "It may not be true but she thought it was true," Maria whispered to her husband. It did not occur to any one there that they were not connoisseurs of modern art, that Baben might have been experimenting with art forms rather than expressing his sexuality. Certainly, Kunjam's maid had no doubts; she had listened long enough to her mistress's recriminations.

"What are you saying?" Kuri was horrified and his arm fell away from her. He threw the drawings from him, "Who would kill my mother?"

"I meant," said Maria, "that it is true what she says...about your father. At least, it's true that your mother thought so, she hinted it to me many times."

"She was killed to stop her telling the truth," shrilled the maid. She leant over them, her face contorted with emotion and spite. "Your grandmother had her killed," she screamed at Kuri, and drops of saliva flew from her mouth and on to Kuri's face. "Everyone heard her threaten to do it. 'I'll stop you if it's the last thing I do,' she said and you all overheard her, you were all standing outside the door when she said it. I saw you."

Kuri rose slowly to his feet, wiping the maid's spit off his face. He looked so forlorn that Maria longed to take him in her arms and comfort him. He looked at her and as their eyes met she felt a thrill of knowing that there was communion between them, that he needed her strength to rely upon. She knew he had idolised his dead and unknown father.

"What shall we do?" he asked bleakly and it was to Maria he addressed the question. "She is talking nonsense, of course," it was almost an appeal.

"There will have to be an investigation, I suppose," Maria answered.

"There must be an investigation," the maid shouted. "If you don't do something about it, I will. My mistress trusted you," she added to Maria, "but she trusted me as well and I will never let her down."

Everyone there knew that an investigation would bring untold trouble. It meant that every unsavoury detail would be pulled out and examined by prying and hostile eyes. It meant scandal and disgrace. The Big House had once had power and prestige enough to manipulate any of the municipal officers. These days, however, as the sons of the Big House often bemoaned, communism had caused many a former untouchable or an upstart of unknown family to rise to positions of power, from which they loved to harass people like those of the Big House, aristocrats, privileged, the once rich and powerful. It was happening everywhere, the low caste avenging years of inhumanity, the low born and landless turning upon the landlords, the privileged. Ellayen, the landless labourer whom Baben had once defended, now had sons-in-law who called themselves by caste names and held positions of power. Even Kunjam's maid who had lived all these years in Big House, was infected with the new trouble making spirit.

They looked at each other in horror and dismay and drew closer to one another in unconscious reflex. Kuri could not help asking himself which was worse, his mother drunkenly falling downstairs (what was she doing up in the attic?) or suicide, especially following his father's suicide and the scandal with Rachie. The maid's allegation of murder he discounted completely. For the moment, any way, he did not question why such an allegation should be made. He was surprised at his feeling of grief and he felt himself in need of comfort; he could not cope with all the rest of it, he could not bear the maid's strident voice. It was not fair that such a thing should have happened to him. He had long wondered whether his father had homosexual leanings but over the years it had ceased to matter to him; he would not want it shouted from the housetop, of course, but he felt neither shame nor anger. It had all ceased long since to matter to him. As poet and artist he tried to understand all human foibles, but no, he did not want it all made public, his family brought into disrepute.

Kunjam's maid waited to see what they were going to do. It was clear to all of them there that she was going to tell everyone that Kunjam had been about to speak about the past and that she had been silenced. Murder! The family shivered almost collectively; although they all felt its impossibility, they knew well what the outside world would make of such a thing. The maid would insist that the old Mistress had hated Kunjam. And it was true. There would be nothing to prove that, invalid though she was, she had not got some other hand to push Kunjam to her death. The wives of the sons of the house moved closer, defensive, to their husbands. What was to be done? Everyone looked at Maria.

When the family descended the attic stairs, picking their way carefully down because many rungs were rotten and uneven, it was to find that the doctor had been sent for. Chacko had suffered one of his heart attacks and the old lady's blood pressure had risen, giving her a nasty turn. The doctor had examined Kunjam's body, pronounced her officially dead. A cloth covered the body and had been pulled over her face. "There will need to be an inquest," the doctor told the men of the Big House. "I cannot sign the death certificate until after that."

Without a death certificate all kinds of complications would arise. It was like a nightmare, but as the sun rose and the rooster ceased its morning crowing, the family came to terms with the fact that they were in the midst of a terrifying crisis; one in which none of them had any idea what to do.

"I will send for Chandy saar," announced Verghese, "he is friendly with all those officials. He will see to it all for us and we will not have to worry."

Chandy saar came willingly. A scandal of this proportion was something to be relished. "See," he told his wife, who had been complaining that he had not attended to the tapioca patch or the cows' lean-to, jobs he had long promised to take in hand, "you think only of petty matters. I am needed for higher things. You women are all alike, unable to rise above the little things of life. But there is far more to life than you even dream of and people like me are needed to attend to them," saying which, he collected his ubiquitous umbrella that accompanied him everywhere, rain or shine, and departed for the Big House. His wife shook her head and went out to attend herself to the tapioca and to the cowshed. It was left to her to say of the dead woman whom she had scarcely known: "Poor woman, may God have mercy on her soul."

The children, Yuhan and Elishuba, stood round-eyed and perplexed by the strange behaviour of the adults. Maria took her children in her arms and tried to explain to them that their grandmother had died during the night. "She is happy now, little ones, she is at peace with no more pain."

"Is she an angel now, standing beside God?" asked Yuhan.

"No silly," replied his twin, before their mother could say anything, "she's lying in the front room and she looks like she's sleeping."

Maria cradled her children in her arms. "Yes," she said firmly, "your grandmother is with the angels in heaven." As she spoke, she smiled in spite of herself. It was hard to imagine Kunjam who for the last thirty years had never been to church, never said a prayer, as a beatific angel. What, she wondered, would God and his angels make of Kunjam? Even as the question formed in her mind and tears rushed to her eyes, she felt strangely comforted.

Almost, she thought she heard Kunjam's irrepressible drunken chuckle.

20

Chandy saar, on his way to the Tahsildar's office, to discuss the question of a death certificate and the avoidance of an inquest, pondered the complexities of the task before him. He considered his alternatives. He knew of the maid's allegations and he discounted them for, as he had said to Verghese: "That class of person loves a good drama. Her mistress has gone, why not squeeze some excitement from it and take her place on the stage? You mark my words, that's all there is to it." His voice was rich with reassurance and his listeners were greatly comforted.

However, there remained the incontrovertible fact of the body at the bottom of the ladder. If she had fallen, was it because she was drunk and if so, would that drunkenness, hitherto veiled, have to be made public? If the fall were not the result of a drunken accident, would it be made out that Kunjam had committed suicide? This was not a particularly respectable alternative for a family such as that of the Big House, but to Chandy saar, man of the world, it seemed as if it could be manipulated to suit their purposes. Careful talk of years of grief following the suicide of Baben, delicate hints about the problems of women of a certain age, a feeling perhaps of redundancy now that her only son was well settled in life. Yes, Chandy saar was definitely inclined to play this card.

Maria had told Kuri that although it might be necessary to enlist Chandy saar's help, certain things must not be revealed to him, lest he in turn, indiscreet, let it all out. She did not have as much confidence in his discretion as the uncles did. Accordingly, the allegations of Baben's errant sexuality had not been revealed to him, nor had he been allowed to speak with the maid; he had also not been permitted to see those strange drawings of fierce, unfeminine women, their genitalia a confusion of erasure and redrawing.

Chandy saar knew that the Coroner was a *Pulaya,* a lower caste, who had risen in government service through a combination of being owed favours, the ability to do favours for those in power and a lack of squeamishness in what he did. He was a dedicated communist. He also revelled in power which manifested itself by keeping people waiting to see him; spending time seemingly lost in his paperwork while his visitors hovered nervously, waiting to be acknowledged.

It took quite five minutes before he raised his eyes from what appeared to be a file with the most riveting contents and became aware of the fact that Chandy saar was standing in front of him. Innocence could be the most telling card of all for it permitted one to speak with compelling honesty about things one would otherwise stumble over, that might stick in the throat. Chandy saar was unburdened by guilty knowledge, so he spoke with eloquence of the horror in the Big House when Kunjam's crumpled body had been discovered; how it had caused Chacko *Thampuraan* to have a heart attack and had laid *Thampuratti*, the Mistress of Big House, low probably never to recover. He saw by the frown on the Coroner's face that his use of the traditional feudal titles had not been well received, but the man nodded his acceptance of the story and Chandy saar was encouraged to go on with his embellishments. He quickly decided that a tone of disrespect towards the Big House family might be preferred. "You know," he said, "what these bourgeois families are like. Everyone instantly went to pieces, had to send for me to see to things. Kuri, the son of the deceased, absolutely useless in a crisis. All I can say is, the poor chap is heartbroken finding his mother like that..."

Veeran, the Coroner, leaned forward: "What was she doing up in the *thattumbaram* at that hour of the night?" His expression was eager and Chandy saar, always ready for a spot of friendly gossip, regretted that he had no juicy tale to unfold, he knew that he might not even hint at any delectable scandal.

"Looking for something belonging to her dead husband," Chandy saar replied smoothly. "You know the fancies women have, there's no predicting what they will get up to. Why, only the other night my wife got up and nothing would do but she must find a notebook in which she had once written down a recipe for a pickle. Kept me awake half the night I can tell you and it is a pickle I don't even much care for."

Veeran nodded. Clearly a familiar chord had been struck here, but he persisted: "There have been rumours. They say the Old Woman has never liked her daughter-in-law, that she blamed her for the son's death."

"Tell me, friend, which mother-in-law really loves her daughter-in-law? And if the son is one's youngest and most loved child it is even more difficult. Then if that son goes and commits suicide who will a mother blame if not the wife?"

"Why did he commit suicide?" asked the indefatigable Veeran.

"Oh, it all happened before my time, but I believe he was an artistic type," here Chandy saar touched his head suggestively, indicating that art and sanity could not be expected to coexist peaceably. "Some say he wanted to marry some other girl who was not suitable. Who knows? Any way, it took place a long time ago."

"I don't know," said Veeran, "it doesn't smell right to me. I think we shall have to look into it. Hold an autopsy."

"Believe me, you will find nothing and you will cause the family untold distress..."

Veeran stiffened: "Are you trying to tell me that we must bypass the rules because of the family's social standing?"

Chandy saar was pained: "Did I say that? Anyone will tell you that I am the most democratic of fellows, total equality and all that. Of course, one must abide by the rules, but we must also consider the old lady's age and that of her poor sons. Already, Chacko has had a heart attack."

"I have heard," the Coroner went on, "that the deceased drank. The toddy tapper from whom she got her drink is related to my wife. If we find alcohol in the body we can say it was an accident. If not, we have to consider suicide and from the things I have heard it seems to me that we have also to think of murder." He leaned back in his chair, well satisfied by this masterly summing up.

"*Aiyo*!" Chandy saar half rose from his chair, a look of extreme shock on his face. "What are you saying? Who would wish to murder her and who in the Big House is capable of such a deed? The Mistress is eighty-five if she's a day and her sons are no chickens either. Not one of them is capable of such a thing, in fact, just between you and me, not one of them is capable of much at all. A bunch of useless people who have outlived their time and place." This last statement was pure genius for it was what Veeran wanted to hear, the Big House and its inhabitants denigrated; now it only remained for Chandy saar to tactfully hand over the money that had been entrusted to him. Nobody had called it a bribe but it was intended to persuade the powers that be that there was no case.

"Money," Verghese had said to him as handed over the cash,

"is a great sweetener. Those low fellows in the Tahsildar's office will jump at such an opportunity." Chandy saar had agreed.

Carefully holding the wedge of money in his palm, Chandy saar leaned over the table and inserted it into a corner of the file nearest him while Veeran looked studiously away. Chandy saar, having got rid of the money so that only a tell tale corner showed, breathed a sigh of relief. All had gone well. He rose to his feet, collected his ubiquitous paraphernalia of walking stick, umbrella and cloth bag and prepared to take his leave. Which was when Veeran, who had gone back to shuffling his papers, ignoring Chandy saar and everyone else in the room, looked up and announced: "We will hold the autopsy without delay."

"*Ai-aiyo*!" Chandy saar could not believe that the combination of genius and money had not worked. "What can I say, sir, to make you believe that you are making a terrible, a tragic mistake?"

The files had once again engrossed Veeran's attention but he condescended to say without looking up at his visitor: "If there is a suicide letter or you can get a signed affidavit, I shall see what I can do."

"Affidavit?" said poor Chandy saar, "signed by whom and what should it say?" He did not dare to make a joke and add that alas, corpses could not sign affidavits to declare that they had fallen accidentally downstairs. Perhaps he could have hazarded being humorous for Veeran shrugged his shoulders and said: "What can I tell you? That is the rule. An affidavit has to be prepared and since the dead lady cannot sign to say she died accidentally, I don't know who can do it. It will all come out in the inquest after we have had the autopsy. Let no one say that we in Veloorkada have one rule for some and another for others. Everyone is equal these days." To mark the fact that the interview was now definitely over, he rang a strident bell which summoned a peon.

"Next," said Veeran in stentorian tones, referring to the bench-loads of people waiting outside his office.

Meanwhile, Mathen had come to the Big House to pay his condolences. On being told of Chandy saar's visit to the Coroner's office and the family's attempts to hush the matter up, he was wholeheartedly of the view that this was the best, the only course of action.

"Nothing is to be gained by allowing old scandal to be aired; nobody will gain and everybody will suffer. Your mother," he said to Kuri, "is dead and nothing can bring her back. You owe it to her and to your family to make sure that everything is tidied away from public eyes."

"But it is not right, *Appa*," Maria remonstrated. "She wanted the truth to be known at last. I believe she threw herself down those steps and she did it to make people think she had been killed. She wanted Grandmother to be blamed. It was her way of taking revenge because she had been ill treated for too long, blamed for something that was not her fault."

"It doesn't matter," replied Mathen, "she was a sick woman

who did not know what she was saying or doing." He repressed the feeling of shock that had risen within him at his daughter's words; what sort of family was this, he wondered, into which he had married his daughter? He chose his words temperately and carefully: "What you have to consider is the name of this family and the legacy you will leave your children. Nothing is to be gained from such revelations but disgrace and heartbreak for the living. Do you want people to talk of Kuri's mother as insane, or do you want people to say that she was murdered by her husband's family? No, of course, you do not wish any of that, so this is the story you will tell: Your mother-in-law fell to her death while trying to carry down a painting by her husband. The painting was rotten, as anyone can see, and it came apart in her hands making her lose her balance. That is all there is to it. I know the Tahsildar, we went to school together, if you wish I shall have a word with him."

He and his mother, Maria senior, also had a word with Kunjam's maid. No one, not even young Maria, ever knew what was said but the maid was silenced. She left Big House, to which she had come as a young girl accompanying the young bride Kunjam and where she had lived for so many unhappy years. Kunjam's maid was told in no uncertain terms that if she said anything, a word out of turn, she would be dealt with by the law. To Maria's surprise, she made no demur and went quietly. Perhaps she knew that the time for fighting, for revenge was over. There was nothing to be gained. Nobody asked where she went. Nobody seemed to care.

So it was that the matter was settled. Veeran was overruled and no autopsy was held, nor were there any tales of menopausal suicide at the matter of fact no nonsense inquest that was held. Maria came forward to say that her mother-in-law had particularly wanted to show her son and daughter-in-law an early painting done by Baben which had been secreted away in the recesses of the attic, that she must have lost her footing when the rotted canvas came apart in her hands, (this explained the disappearance of the grotesque pictures the family had found in the attic) or tripped over a loose floor board (and there were many such) and lost consciousness.

Maria grieved that she had denied Kunjam her last request, although she recognised that to have done otherwise would have plunged the family into chaos. But, even more, she sorrowed over the fact that poor Kunjam's mind should have been allowed to become so warped that she could stage such a monstrous melodrama. Why had she failed to see the way her mother-in-law's mind had been working? She could not forgive herself.

"I ought to have seen it," she cried to Kuri. "I should have realized when she talked of poison and bolted her door in the middle of the day, that her mind was becoming unhinged. We all failed her and she trusted me. It is that I cannot bear. In the name of respectability, of the family she hated, we have let her down and that means she died in vain. Everyone in the house is happy because his or her skin has been saved. It has always been like that, hasn't it?"

"Maria," said Kuri, "your father is right, it is the living we have to consider. My grandmother cannot be branded a murderer, that is as absurd as it is tragic and our family name cannot be dishonoured..."

"But don't you see that it has been dishonoured because we have all allowed this to happen? Your mother may not have been murdered by anyone but she died because of what this family did to her, starting with your father."

"I will not have you say anything about my father. He was unhappy enough..."

"That's what I mean," Maria interrupted, "if only he had the courage to say no to marriage, to follow his path, none of this would have happened."

"You don't know what you are saying," Kuri's voice was weary and Maria went to him and put her arms around him and Kuri leaned against her.

He spoke softly so that she had to lean over him to hear: "We are not all brave and sure of ourselves, able to take whatever path we want at any cost.... My poor father was just a sad, mixed up person who did not know how to deal with who or what he was. Perhaps he felt he had to assert his normality, perhaps my mother was the wrong woman for him, who knows? And now we never will. All I know is, nothing will be achieved by washing our dirty clothes in public."

Maria said nothing, just went on stroking his head, but she thought to herself: 'Once again it is the Big House that has survived at the expense of everyone else.'

She was learning that death was accompanied not only by loss and grief, it was jostled by guilt. Guilt for all those moments of anger or exasperation when one had turned away, all those moments one had not shared, when sympathy or joy had not been offered. We always imagine there would be a tomorrow, a new beginning, an opportunity for reparation or solution: 'After all,' said Maria to herself, 'we could not live otherwise.' But death ended everything; a sharp truncation, and we would be left with a burden of unspoken words, emotions that could never be expressed. There was contrition, Maria realised, but there could be no expiation. Of all sad words of tongue and pen, the saddest were 'it might have been'. What would Kunjam have been, had she tasted happiness?

21

Maria knew that she had betrayed Kunjam, but she recognized that it had to be done for the sake of the family. For all of them, for her children. It surprised her that she had so soon joined what might be termed the Establishment, but to be rebellious and stir up trouble is not so easy when one has children and a husband to consider. Nor was it any longer possible to cast Kuri's grandmother in a villainous role, created for her by Kunjam as her last revenge and which, up to a point, remembering her own grandmother's treatment in Big House, Maria had subscribed to. Although she had once hated her, remembering her grandmother's stories of the beatings with broomsticks, the hot sweet balls, those were faraway days and she now saw the erstwhile mistress of Big House only as a weak old woman who had endured much. A woman whom, oddly, Maria had come to admire for her strength of character and with whom, unconsciously, she identified herself. Her feelings for the old woman were different from those she had felt towards Kunjam, although it was the latter she had loved.

Feeling the guilt of betrayal, Maria needed something or someone to blame. Why did there have to be so many secrets? So many so-called norms from which little or no deviation was allowed? Somewhere, perhaps, there was a place where people could love those of their own sex and fear neither reprisal nor scorn; where women could seize love on their own terms and not be known as harlots, shameless. Poor Baben and Kunjam; the one forced to live a life perhaps of concealment, more likely of disappointment, that had become unbearable, the other with a lust for life, starved to death, until her warped mind could only fashion bizarre revenge. Who was actually to blame for it all? Not the old grandmother, for like everyone else she was a product of her time and society and how many have the courage, the willingness and the ability to change society? Maria was realizing that it was not easy, nor even always possible, to have a clear-cut choice.

The sand was running out for the old grandmother, she was slowly but surely losing her grip on life. In a kind of delirium she tossed and turned upon her bed and cried out frequently. The names most often on her lips were Baben and Kunjam. "I wanted to kill her, did I kill her, did I?" she cried once, starting up. With a firm hand Maria made her lie down again, while the faithful Chauathi put cooling cloths on her forehead and unceasingly massaged her legs. "She will be gone soon," the old servant said, "and then it will all end... finally." She looked at Maria: "It is time for a new beginning," she added.

But it took a long and painful time for the old woman to die. Repeatedly, Maria asked herself whether Kunjam was just a weak person who had been driven, as weak people so often were, to desperate action; weak people in their desperation often did foolish things. Or was she really tough and calculating, intent on revenge; she had made scenes enough before she died, perhaps they had all been part of her plan...

Or, was it possible that someone had been used to push Kunjam to her death? The very old sometimes became ruthless, had less concern about life and death. No! Maria shook herself, that way madness lay. The guilt the old grandmother felt, causing her to start up in her sleep, was due to the fact that she knew she was morally responsible.

With Kunjam's passing, Maria realized that there was no one in the Big House in whom she might confide, no one who spoke and thought as Kunjam had. She felt as if she were suddenly inwardly dumb with no more words to express what she felt; for those words had been Kunjam's, words that had struck chords within her, arousing emotions that might never again surface, remaining like subterranean fish in the deeper waters of her mind.

Kuri would never know her as she had begun to know herself; but then, did she, would she know him as he perhaps wanted to be known? Did many people, she wondered, ever break through their bonds and reach each other in true union? Perhaps instead, Maria thought sadly, we leave each other largely undiscovered. Like a fisherman coasting the waters, catching fish, but unaware of all that teemed under the bright water, taking from it only that which he considered he needed, glad of the flashes of silver in his net. In the moments following Kunjam's death Kuri had turned instinctively to her and a link had been forged, one of many, and Maria knew that new and other bonds would tie them ever closer to one another. Kuri was one of those who would always need other people to take care of life's problems for him. It struck Maria that most of the people of the Big House (apart from the old mistress who had been strong) were that way, relying on others to smooth their passage, to attend to the rigours of living. They were different from people like her grandmother Maria, strong and self-reliant, or her father, even herself, people who took life by the horns and subdued it to their own ends.

It wasn't, thought Maria, who one was that was important; what was really important was what one was. Family and name, prestige and power were all very well, but finally all that matters was one's ability to stand up to life. This seemingly simple fact had never been grasped by the Big House family and if Kuri had grasped it, he nevertheless repined that life had not given him the ability to deal better with its slings and arrows. Such people, thought Maria, always blamed others, never their own weakness.

The Big House had endured and would endure on the strength of its women, people like Kuri's grandmother and herself, its custodians and its prisoners. Like them, Maria had energy and she had a desire to be doing. The reins of the Big House passing, imperceptibly at first, into her keeping, she had found that she identified herself with the house. She had become determined to put it on as firm a financial keel as possible, to leave a proper inheritance for her children and her children's children. It was amazing how soon a house such as the Big House brought out one's dynastic leanings.

Maria constantly looked about for ways in which she could further shore up the prosperity of the Big House. She had hoped at first that this would draw her and Kuri closer, make them united in a common purpose, but she had soon discovered that Kuri like all the other males in the family, wanted only to live well, not concern himself with the mechanics of drudgery. After Kunjam's death she needed more than ever something with which to occupy herself.

Maria had inherited her father's business acumen and she had the shrewdness, thrift and industriousness of all her forebears. She could not understand Kuri's lack of interest. When she had gone to him one day with a scheme to grow mangosteen, a fruit much prized in south east Asia and one that she felt sure would grow easily on their estate, she had been lit up with enthusiasm, spoken of export potential, of a money spinner. But "Do what you like!" had been Kuri's response and it had been like a door closing in her face. Perhaps he had seen that for he had added, as if in extenuation, "I think business is boring and I have no interest in it."

He had been bent over his notebook writing, Maria was sure, another of his numerous poems, some of which were published in obscure journals that she had never heard of and were sometimes reviewed in others equally unknown to her. They were as boring to her as her business ventures were to him.

Her husband's poems did not speak to her, indeed she was hard pressed to know what, if anything, they were about. They certainly earned him no money and Maria was, after all, her father's daughter; she believed in profit and loss and with the latter she had little patience. She resented it the more because she believed that Kuri used his poetry to shut her out, to make her feel inferior. That she could not appreciate his poems gave him the right to feel superior and he was able to relegate her business acumen to the world of the practical, the humdrum, although it was what kept him and Big House going.

While coming to terms with her dissatisfaction with so many aspects of her life, it had never occurred to Maria to complain to her father and grandmother who had arranged this marriage for her. She loved them too much to pain them with her feelings which, anyway, changed often, assuming new forms so that she was never sure enough of herself to be able to judge if the fault lay with her. Protected, as she had been all her young life, Maria knew little or nothing about how things ought to be between a man and a woman, or even (looking at the fractured and separate lives around her) whether it was of great importance. In any case, the way she looked at it, her life was hers and she had to, she knew, battle for it herself. There was no use repining, apportioning blame.

As she was to tell her daughter Elishuba many years later: "I was not only innocent, I was undemanding. At first I never thought that one has a claim on life. I did not know either how or what to demand of life except for what one is told one can have and the truth is, you get only what you demand from life. The trouble is, most of us don't have any idea of the scope we have."

Being inexperienced, Maria was ready enough to acknowledge that the fault, if any, might lie with her. So she had thrown herself into her business schemes and as with her father, they flourished and she made money. Perhaps, after all, she was not much different from her husband's grandmother; or maybe the house fashioned her as it had the other. They were women not easily satisfied, women with men who could not entirely satisfy.

In the end, the house claimed Maria as it had claimed the women before her. The house contained them as no husband had; it was cherished while it challenged and occupied their waking thoughts. At night it held them and wove itself into their dreams. It was the past that women clung onto, but it was also the future. That meant that nothing had been wasted. Life would go on.

Sometimes the house stirred as if with a life of its own, as indeed it had, as all old houses do. Maria sighed in her sleep and turned and tossed, aware of many things that were beyond the reach of her waking mind.

Her children, Elishuba and Yuhan, rediscovered Big House and made it their own. Old anecdotes, told and retold, touched upon their minds and fragmenting, became legend, indistinct from the fairy stories they were told, the tales they later read. Old hiding places opened anew before them and corners of the house and garden that had delighted children of a bygone time became the delight of these two. And it was all new, undiscovered, theirs alone, until the next generation and the next took possession of it and made it theirs.

Time in the Big House stood still, its generations indistinguishable, like so many successive waves breaking upon the sand, ever rolling, never stopped. And the Big House continued, surmounting its many tragedies, absorbing its happiness into its very fabric and it seemed as if it would always be there. If there were ghosts, they troubled nobody; the old women, Kuri's grandmother and her faithful maid who followed her into death, did not haunt Big House. If Kunjam's spirit endured in Big House, it was a benign presence, her influence reaching out in many ways that freed Maria and enabled her to set her daughter Elishuba free to do what she wanted, achieve what she could. Sometimes Maria thought of how it might have been and wondered sadly what it would have been like if she and, even more, Kunjam before her, had tasted real happiness.

Together, the twins banished the darkness that had enveloped Baben and Kunjam and they faced their separate futures with confidence and with joy. When Yuhan began to paint with a facility, and the old uncles and aunts said reminiscent of Baben, no ghosts surfaced; it was simply a family gift that had been passed on, devoid of the twisted agony that had gone before.

The old breadfruit tree, on which poor Baben had hanged himself on that long ago rainy afternoon, never did bear fruit again. But a seed dropped by a bird on the wing took root and crept its way up the old tree trunk and a new tree began to flourish on the bare stump.